# s...toieburg

Andre Zemnovitsch

**author**HOUSE®

*AuthorHouse*™
*1663 Liberty Drive*
*Bloomington, IN 47403*
*www.authorhouse.com*
*Phone: 1-800-839-8640*

*First published by AuthorHouse 2/10/2011*

*ISBN: 978-1-4567-1704-9 (sc)*
*ISBN: 978-1-4567-1836-7 (e)*

*Library of Congress Control Number: 2010918693*

*Printed in the United States of America*

# Dedication

To my family, my best friend Mr. Paul Sukholinskiy, my friend,right-hand man and illustrator Mr.Raphael Tomkin, and my editor and friend Miss.Tess Baldwin. You all are my muses and I am eternally obliged to all of you.

"The mind is its own place and in itself, can make a Heaven of Hell, a Hell of Heaven."

John Milton

" I'm all about being Ironic but don't admit it."

Some random Hipster tool

# s.. Up ?

I felt their respect for me fall by the wayside as my bloodshot eyes sank into the meandering darkness. At one frail point of my life, reality was simply a preposterous entity; I serenaded perception the same way a playboy seduces a woman. I took to heart all the idiosyncratic nonsense that would identify me as a person, rather than just admit I'm a bacterial presence floating around in some deity's masterminded microcosm. "Fuck the chess players," my father would often rant in his Gin soaked tangents. "Those who think more than one step ahead are merely a bunch of protozoan conmen who merely strive to fathom." To fathom means to understand, how can we understand anything if nothing is written in stone, and if it is, who's to tell me the stone is there in the first place? "Play checkers son, concentrate on the now, not the what if." Took pops' advice to heart and decided to take a gamble. Living in Vermont was nothing short of wholesome. Dad being the fairly wealthy investment banker that he was, and step-mom being the jaded, apathetic cunt she was, made life, well, more or less pleasurable. Friday nights consisted of gallivanting around with my inner clique and partaking in a myriad of drugs running the gamut from Acid to Zoloft. None of us ever "shot the rig" because that would be stigmatic. Shooting anything or smoking crack-cocaine were pretty much the only two taboos that my idiot friends and I refrained from doing. We were living happily in our rationalized world where it was copasetic to drink, snort, smoke, drop, or pop something, well anything for that matter, but never inject anything. Crack was a no because only the poor swine of society used it. We were too good and way too pretty for that vermin poison. Yes, life was good, so the only justifiable course of action was to get up and leave ole Vermont. I was destined for bigger and better things. Vermont was getting tedious and as much as I enjoyed our romps and mesmerizing interludes with lady psychedelia, I felt that leaving here was the key to me figuring out who and what I was. Truth be told, I never traveled, always having the time and resources, i.e. daddy, but fancied lounging around and smoking a nice joint. Once in a while we would take impromptu road trips to Vermont's 69 buddy, New Hampshire, but that was as far as we went. When I told Dad that I was moving to New York City, his lack of emotions made me cringe. He always preached that men should be stoic, but c'mon old man, your son is moving away for the first time and who knows if and when you'll see him again. I wanted to screech "callous bastard" in his face like a banshee scorned, but quickly realized that his financial support was the only lifeline that I had left. "Alright kiddo," he said, "'I'll wire you eight hundred smackeroos every week. Stay safe and remember to stay away from the minorities!" The old man really was a Racist WASP douche bag. I've never been to NYC but subconsciously knew it would be the haven I desired. On the day I left, I felt I looked rather spiffy in my plaid shirt and semen-exterminating skinny jeans. I put on my trusty ole Tortoise shell Ray-bans ala Bob Dylan circa 1968 and caught the first bus heading to Manhattan. Bon Voyage!!

## EHH, HOW YOU say... BRIGHTON BEACH...

Since I didn't have a pad to call my own yet in the Big Apple, my first destination was anywhere that I could crash a few nights in. luckily my buddy Vlad had what was referred to by the local derelicts as a decent "crib," and was kind enough to let me spend some time there. He lived on Brighton and 4th street in a nice little two bedroom spot. Vladdy didn't take any cash from me for letting me stay over, but he sure as fuck didn't deny the free Grey Goose and quality coke I brought. So, seeing as though I'm not from around here, the mere fact that Brighton was a beach got me excited, until I actually saw the beach itself. My friends, Brighton beach sits gracelessly amidst the shit-stained Anus of the Atlantic Ocean. It is hugged by Sheepshead Bay and Coney Island. The sand is an atrocious collaboration of glass and fecal matter. The broken corona bottles glistening in the sun add a certain compliment to the Blunt clippings and used tampon dispensers muddled in the sand. All five senses are completely shell-shocked when first stepping out here.

You try your ever-so-hardest to not to pull an Oedipus Rex and gouge your corneas out from witnessing 80 year old "babushkas" parading around thinking that they can pull off two-piece itsy bitsy teeny-weeny yellow Juicy bikini's, with SLUT printed on their ass crack. Your ears are scolded by intangible Russian and English profanities known colloquially as "Brighton beach Russian." "Pashyul nahuy petarasd" was the first thing the fine ole quasi-Mafioso told me when I naively asked him how the water was. Translated: Go fuck yourself Faggot! The smell is overwhelmingly ineffable. Words can't quite describe what the nasal cavities experience. Luckily for me, my septum is deviated, thanks to the devil's dandruff, so it wasn't as God-awfully pungent as what it should've been. My taste buds were then pummeled by eating a Brooklyn staple known as a Nathan's famous hot dog, which is basically a hot dog consisting of every entrails of the animal that normal people can't stomach. I believe it was Gorbachev that said that "there is no such thing as Russian cuisine. Russian cuisine is whatever food tastes good with Vodka." No shit, these liverless titans drink so much alcohol I would have to be in the clutches of an epic hunger frenzy to stomach this carnie drek! Let's see that is sight, sound, smell, and taste. As for touch, that is one sense I didn't really experience. Simply put, I really didn't feel like touching anything or anyone. As the setting sun penetrates the haze of Dante's Inferno, this lower circle of debauchery, the night comes creeping along nonchalantly in my peripheral vision. Nights in BB are better witnessed in person. Otherwise, my claims would seem farfetched and downright unbelievable. If a visionary artist would imagine and attempt to portray the proverbial downward spiral they would paint something along the lines of BB at night. "This is where hookers come to die," my friend Vlad grunted, and squealed, making a parabolic exaggeration with his hand, sweeping the panoramic horizon of Brighton. I felt somewhat secure walking with a crowd of five locals as we marched on to our destination, a good drinking joint Vlad had suggested on Brighton 1st street. The walk from Brighton 7th to Ocean Parkway, at the end of BB, consisted of walking under the Q and B train lines. As if the general ambience isn't already downright treacherous with the Mafia men, drunks, and vagabonds on streets, the deafening roar of the train directly overhead makes a bad Acid trip look like Disney Land. As we walk on to our watering hole all cheeched out and barely out of the k-hole, we pass one of the infinite bordellos that line the corners. Vlad tells me that I'm not a true blue New Yorker until I chug my first 40. Truth be told, I had no idea what a 40 was. These fuckers are crazy, I thought. A 40 could be anything from a game of Russian roulette to Heroin, but taking my Dad's advice, I was stoic and didn't think too much of it. There is a fine line between being stoic and being completely numb, but fuck it! To my chagrin, a 40 was simply forty ounces of shitty malt liquor that the local hoodlums consumed to get drunk faster. I smirked and chugged the bottle in a few minutes: easy peezy son! As we kept walking, something caught my eye. Under the faint opalescent glimmer of the "Apteka" (pharmacy sign); I thought that I had spotted someone lying half-naked in the gutter. I inched closer, and sure as fuck there she was. My friends, at first hesitant to approach the urchin, became enthused due to the fact that it was a girl lying there. She was not too bad looking, if I say so myself, but that is meaningless to me, seeing as I refuse to have sex, ever! I'll get into that later. Though I could see my buds were contemplating having their way with this little tramp, lucidity quickly set in as they realized the repercussions of doing said action. No, they couldn't give two flying fucks about whether or not it was legal because they were all well

5

connected. Instead, all of them were clean for the most part, and who knows what hybrid STD's have been manifesting in this chick. They backed off as I inched closer and closer to observe her. Again, there was absolutely no sexual desire on my part, just my voyeuristic tendencies. I couldn't help grinning and chuckling a bit as I observed her. Staring at her, I spotted the three colors that symbolize our great nation and modern Americana, quintessential patriotism. There was red, the color of the blood serenading down towards her upper lip, white, the color of the dried up semen stains zigzagging all around her blouse and blue, the color of the throbbing veins jetting out in all directions across her arm, like some sort of schematic of the complex NYC subway system. Daddy's little patriot, I murmur inaudibly to myself, as I attempt to wipe off some miscellaneous fluid gushing out of one of her facial crevasses. Her gaze is constant with mine. Her nostrils are pulsating, her brow is furrowed and her lip is quivering, but her crystallized retinas remain pinpointed on mine. "Kak tybya Zavut?" Vlad asks her assuming she's Russian. "Sveta," she hisses as she makes a failed attempt to stand up. My buds find this most entertaining. "You're a regular lamb of God, aren't ya dear?" Vlad asks her. "More of a hecatomb," I chime in, getting a few cheap laughs from the flock. I felt like a whore saying that! I assist her, being careful not to come in contact with anything seeping from her skin. I lean her against the wall and tell her to stay safe and that this city will eat you alive. She laughs in my face, as if knowing I'm not from around here. "Who the fuck are you telling me anything you schmuck?" I remain quiet, and join up with the buds to go pound a few shots. This experience had left a bad taste in my mouth. I wake up the next morning, well in the afternoon technically, hung over as usual, and decide that it is finally time to look for my own place. I give Vlady the remnants of the 8-ball I had bought the other night and set out to find somewhere where I belong, somewhere more like....

# WILLIAMS... FUCKING BURG!!! (

As soon as I stepped foot on Roebling street, I knew that this was the place for me. Vlad decided to accompany me. I was most obliged for his consideration but didn't care much for his derogatory anti-hipster quips. No more Versace suits, Adidas sweat suits, or Chanel handbags around here. Everybody looks just like me. It is like some genius scientist had cloned me thousands and thousands of times. Skinny jeans, flannel, ironic t-shirts, and dollar shades make up the large majority of Willyburg. It's Fucking great! "Fuck this bro, I can't stand it here. I'm going back to Brighton where I belong, hit me up if anything kid." It didn't take the realtor long to convince me to lease the loft she had picked out. It cost $2,300 a month with utilities, and I could easily do that. I sign the contract, and she pours me a flute of Dom Perignon to celebrate my moving in. "Welcome to NYC kiddo, you're going to fit in just fine around here." "Sure am, ma'am," I tell her, and make my way downstairs. As I look around and decide on which one of the myriad of bars to go to, I see a group of large men petitioning something. "Fuck Hipsters!" "Have Williamsburg and Greenpoint annexed to Manhattan" "BK needs no BS," and a plethora of other Bensonhurstian themed anti-demographical chants are prevalent amongst this crowd of overfed, wife beater donning Neanderthals. I shrug my shoulders as a couple of these beasts throw some obscene slander my way and I leave. As I arrive at the Crocodile Lounge, the scene is noticeably more copasetic then the episode I had just encountered outside. Here, there is no harassment, no animosity, no fat! There is simply a congregation of peeps that get me for me. A conversation is as easy to start here as a VD is easy to catch in Jersey, nothing complicated just me swigging my PBR and going with the flow. What really strikes me as awesome is the array of music that is being played via the jukebox. Great contemporary bands that I dig are belting their tunes: MGMT, Vampire Weekend and Metric, to name a few. Williamsburg is esthetically pleasing, and quite different from what I had seen in BB. It sounds good, it smells good, the gourmet lumberjack food here is awesome, and the feel is sublime. I go to the bathroom to do a few bumps of K off of my key and run into this anorexic looking chick. "Hey studly, I'll let ya suckle my teeties for some of that powda of yours." I giggle a bit. "I'll just give ya some, no reciprocation necessary." "Ooh, I'm sorry love, I thought ya played for the other team, didn't think ya were gay" "I'm not ma'am," I sigh, "I just don't fancy anything sexual." "Yeah, yeah, and I'm a Vegan," at which point she bites down on a Slim Jim she's holding. "So seriously, what's the deal? Were you like touched as a child or something?" "Nope, I just never liked physical contact." "Alright Howie Mandel, I'm sorry. I was just attempting to be polite." "No harm, sweetie. I'm not gay, I'm not bi. I'm just me. I find it is more beneficial to concentrate on just being than it is to consistently crave sexual acts." "That's cool. So you're like Morrissey, eh?" "No, I'm not gay!" "Oh so you're like Clyde from Bonnie and Clyde, is that it?" "No, I'm not impotent." "Ok, Ok, I give up. My name is Raya. Listen, so a couple of my girls and I are having this soiree over at my pad later. Feel free to bring your non-sexual self over, it starts around 11 tonight" "Sure, why not? That sounds awesome. I actually just moved in, and would love to get to know a few heads around here, so sweet, I'll see ya then." "Ciao, mi amore." "Oh, by the way my name..." "Shh, I don't care. You will be known as Mr. Sniffles from now on." I fucking love Williamsburg! I go back to the bar, grab a few more PBRs and make my way back to my loft. It is 9:45PM already, and I need at least an hour to look like I don't give a shit what I look like. I get to Raya's door at 11:54 sharp, not too repulsively late, but not quite fashionably late, just plain late. "Shoulda came a bit earlier, Mr. Sniffles," Raya yells out to her posse, laughing in the background. "Ya, sorry hun, it took me a while to find your pad." "It's cool. Ya want some Acid? It's ill, my boy Skids just brought it over from Cali." "Fuck yeah! I'll take five hits." I wanted to show her us New Englander VMONT boys can out party the New Yorkers. This was a bad idea on my behalf. A few hours later, I wake up. I'm naked, cold, and feel torn. Shit, dye my hair black and call me Natalie Imbruglia! My pale English body is laid out in some sort of "dawn of the dead" position. Romero would've been proud. A few feet from reach is my baggie, my precious baggie with the little ketamine I still had left. Aside from a couple of residual minor hallucinations, the LSD trip had ceased. I mosey over to the bathroom and wash myself up a tad. Damn, I look like a fucking troll. As I sober up a little in front of the mirror, many of the idiosyncratic details that I had during my trip come into perspective. The first thing I remember is receiving a sloppy blowjob from Raya. A combination of her ceaseless bargaining and the five hits of Monterey purple were enough to let the id have its way. Then I realize that my ass hurts. What the Hell!?!? Was I fucked in the ass? As I try hard to recall, I realize that I had fallen off the couch onto one of Raya's action figures, so even though there was no flesh-light penetrating my boy hole, G.I. Joe went to town on me. Fucking don't ask don't tell my ass! I pivot my hip, and see something written on my back. It is pretty long. I do remember that the girls used me as an easel. I go over to Raya's room, and find her crouched in some Yoga position. She is waiting for me with a smirk from ear to ear and a bottle of KY lube. "What is written on my back, Raya?" "Oh, just something I thought was pretty cool when I was peaking. Want me to read it for ya babe?" "That would be nice." "Standing on the zenith with consciousness in my rear view mirror I squander the remaining remnants of my god given humanity and embark on my predestined journey. The harmonization of colors and shapes mesmerize every fiber of my being, or lack thereof in this scenario. The hairs on the back of my neck rise are askew, in positions as if ready to march. The senses interweave with one another, stopping any chance of dissipation by symbiotically feeding off of one another's mannerisms." "Wow! How fucked up were we, love? Jeez, to come up with something like that is uncanny. Maybe you should become a writer or something." "No babe, it's something a dear friend of mine wrote years ago when she and I did Ayuasca in the Amazon. That was just months before, well, she left us." "What happened? Did she move out of state or something?" "No love, she died saving her idiot boyfriend's life. After Saffy and I had got back from Brazil, her idiot, chauvinist pig of a boyfriend insisted on taking her on a weekend rendezvous to upstate New York. You see, the fucktard was nothing more than a coked-out adrenaline junkie. Stupid shit had just made his first thousands extorting for the local Guidos and decided to live the high life. So when I was away, he bought a new Sl-500 Mercedes-Benz, fully loaded and chromed out of course, and took Saffy with him. Doing about an 8-ball of quality Nicaraguan white and drinking a bottle of Patron exacerbated his already reckless state of mind. As he was driving 120 miles per hour down Route 17 towards Binghamton, Saffy must have tried to calm him down. Long story short, he must've had turned his head and didn't see the truck trying to merge into his lane. The fucking inbred hillbilly driving the rig was probably even more tweaked out then he was. Next thing he knew, he had woken up the next day, barely conscious. He asked the physicians what had happened, and they told him that it was a miracle he was still alive and not even paralyzed. He asked where Saffy was and the Doc shook his head and told him that she must've inherently sensed the incoming impact and merged herself smack dab between the wheel and the Guido's body just moments before impact. She was in pieces!" "Oh my God, that's, that's, that's..." "At her funeral, the fuck was clearly shaken up. It was a small, serene ceremony. My sister and I read this poem we wrote as her eulogy, while the whole time starring into that fucker's face." "May I hear it?" "We titled it 'Emerald Dragonfly,' and it goes like this: My love and I dance aimlessly in the abyss in almost complete darkness and tranquility. All is silent but the footsteps of our maneuvers. All is blind but the faint shimmer of a green dragonfly perched on a not so distant precipice. Our dance lacks harmony and synchronization. It is more of a judo match than a waltz. I push my love towards the neon sparkle as she counters and proceeds to fling me towards the light. The final petite jeté will determine the outcome. Like a narcoleptic, my love drops to the floor. With a last dose of momentum, she pushes me into the gleaming light that gets brighter as I open my eyes and find myself in a white room. I pivot my head, and see my love catatonic by my side. With one final petty zigzag, the line goes flat, as the dragonfly beats its wings one final time." I was speechless for the better part of thirty minutes after listening to what Raya had shared with me. The passion in her voice, the shivering of her hands, and the perspiration beading on her forehead made me think of two things: just how passionate this angel before me was, and just how much of a numb sociopath my father is. Prior to heading back to my loft I decided to stop by this bar that Raya had recommended. This was the quintessential dive bar with sawdust on the floor, a bathroom worthy of Sing-Sing, and only three beers on tap. Yes, this is my kind of place. The barkeep at this watering hole is a Williamsburg staple. Everyone refers to him as Mr. Mojo. Fittingly enough, as soon as I came into the bar, the Doors were playing on the jukebox and Morrison was belting Mr. Mojo Risin'. Mr. Mojo-the-barkeep was in his late thirties with grizzled, big old spectacles and carrying a gut that was his proud accumulation of 25 years of feasting on munchies. "Eh, here's another skinny jean wearing hip-douche. What can I get ya, dude? Let me guess, a PBR. Right, junior?" "Ha ha, ya that would be great. Say can I ask ya a question mate?" "Sure, as long as you tip well." "So what traumatic event was responsible for you becoming this curmudgeon I see before me?" "So who the fuck do you think you are kid, asking me this shit? Ya don't know me, and ya will never know me! Now take your hipster swill and fuck off!" "I'm sorry man; I'm still tripping a tad from earlier. Say, lemme buy you a shot. I'm sorry for offending ya." "Buy me a shot eh? I'm Irish, ya fucker, ya gotta buy me at least five!" "Ha ha, no problemo dudesky. What'll be?" "Hmm... well, Johnny Walker blue sounds good." "Ok brother man, what's the damage?" "That'll be three hundred bones please." "What the fuck?!? That's ridiculous man!" "Hey you asked for it, hip douche." "Alright, I'll play your game man, but I'm sure as fuck not tipping ya for this PBR!" "Ha! No problem Junior. I own this joint anyhow, that's three bills in my wallet. Woo Atlantic City here I come." Fucking slick wanker! Nine PBRs and two pseudo-flashbacks later were enough for me to finally get up the stamina to go back to my loft. I got back, popped two sticks of Xanax and dosed off to the land of slumber with a smile on my face.

# Me + Me + Chelsea =
# HEADACHEEEE!!

I received three calls and 24 text messages from my pops, asking me how my job hunt was going. "I don't know old timer, I'm not one to prognosticate anything. Remember what you told me about not playing Chess?" "Yeah, yeah, but what if I drop dead today? You have absolutely no talents, no skills and no knowledge of how to survive without Daddy's assistance." That really hit a sore spot for me. I knew the tool was right but I really didn't feel like admitting it. The world is my oyster and I'm living in the greatest city in the world, NYC baby. Oddly enough, I still had all of Manhattan to explore, so I gave Raya a buzz and asked her if she'd wanted to be my designated metropolitan Sherpa. She laughed hysterically and told me that she had the perfect place to take me to in the city. "It would be the ultimate place for you to come out of my shell" "Sure," I said. "This is your city, love, lead the way" I met up with Raya at the Lorimer Street L train station. The L is Williamsburg's answer to Brighton Beach's Q. "So here's what were going to do, noob. First we're gonna take the L to Union Square, then we're gonna walk a few blocks into Chelsea. You can walk in those sized 27 skinny's right?" "Shut the fuck up biatch, ya know it!""Cool beans, you're gonna totally dig this joint. I have this gut feeling that you might even meet your soul mate there." "Alright, sounds legit Raya, I can't wait." Of course the cunt took me to the epicenter of homosexuality. "See, sweetums told ya you'll love it here." "I told ya biatch, I'm not gay!" "Oh yeah you are. No straight man can pass up an ass like mine, and you did. I basically had to beg you to let me give ya one of my famous blowjobs." "Whatever. I'll amuse you. I guarantee I can get at least 10 numbers within the first hour here." "With an ass like that, I have no doubt ya can." The club that Raya and I entered was, for better or worse, extravagant. Coked out boy-toys were grinding perverted older rich gents, while middle-aged average looking men were pulling out every trick in their arsenal to catch an attractive one-night fuck. This place was so fucking fake that it was real. Of course, the cute, young, tall VMONT lad was on the radar of just about every guy in this joint. Though the gay culture is its own sub-tier of society, it is then divided into a bunch of smaller gay demographics. You have the "twinks" who are young, under 25 year old boys, with only hair on their head. Every other body part and orifice is smooth as a baby's bottom. The "bears" are the older, hairy, stocky men who prowl the night searching for prey to call their own. The "pigs" are the dirty men who partake in all the kinky sexual acts that would have them crucified in other countries. The gay lexicon is vast and sometimes frightening once you decipher what the words mean: water sports, scat play, bukkake, rimming, to name a few. But, as seemingly filthy and deranged as the gay culture may seem to close-minded douches, basically everybody in the Bible belt, it too is a delicate microcosm. As the ninth guy approaches and attempts to pick me up,

Raya is losing all hope that I am queer. Judging from her subtle disappointment in me being straight, I can clearly see how upset she is for me not finding her fuckable. Guy number nine goes off, upset like the other eight as a sudden feeling of sorrow comes over me for making Raya feel unattractive. "C'mon love, it's been nice but let's get out of here, eh?" "Yeah Sniffy, guess you weren't kidding, ya really are straight." "I am, but I'm really not physically attracted to anyone, I hope you can understand that. You're a beauty, but I have this thing about not fucking, I'm more drawn to the camaraderie between people, not the physical aspect of it. Intercourse is a weakness, it's an addiction. I don't care how mature and experienced ya are, once you fuck somebody the synergy between the two of you is never the same." "It makes sense, I'm just saddened to hear somebody so young and cute preaching abstinence." As we leave the club, I receive many a dirty stare from the clientele. "Tease," the bouncer hissed. He was actually guy number two who had tried to pick me up to no avail. "C'mon Sniffy, I gots this awesome Thai place we can go to. Are ya hungry?" "Fuck yea I'm hungry, let's go boo." The place was only a block away. It was a great little spot: cheap, stinky, and with a pretty mellow ambiance. I ordered the traditional Satay, while Raya went with the Snapper. "Hmm, that's funny Sniffy. Look over there. That guy is dressed exactly like ya." As I turned around to my delight, the kid really was wearing the same attire as me. My infamous skinny jeans, a green Kurt Cobain style woolly flannel, and my precious Bob Dylan shades. "What the Fuck Sniffy, ya didn't tell me ya had an evil twin." "He's not my twin he's my son! Ya see Raya, I'm really from the future and I'm here to save you and my son from the machines." "Ha ha, Ok Arnold, why don't ya go chat a bit with your son?" "Sure, why not?" He seems all lonesome sitting there by himself. I'll make his day.

1

Before I had any chance to tell my twin chap hello, he gazed square into my eyes and said, "So which one of us is Danny DeVito?" It took me a moment to get the 'Twins' reference, but I laughed and told him it was probably me. "Name's Dominic, but ya can call me whatever ya want stud." "Nice to meet ya Dom, my na…" "That's unimportant. I'm going to call ya Sniff!" "What the fuck?! Has Raya put ya up to this?" "Ha ha, nah dude, I just get the feeling that you're one hell of a cheech aficionado." "Ha! Wow, I'm starting to get a reputation in NYC already!" "Hey, just out of curiosity, have ya ever tried modeling before?" "No, but I was actually thinking of giving it a shot. You're not the first person to tell me I should give it a go." "Here, take this, it's my agents' card. Maybe you and I will do some brother-brother type of shtick." "Yeah, most def brosky. Say, what ya got planned for tonight? Raya and I are planning to paint this town red." "What are ya, some sort of 1940's detective? Paint the town red, ha ha. But yeah, sure, I'm always down for a fun night out on the promenade." "Promenade? You're making fun of me aren't ya Dom?" "Yeah, but just a little. C'mon, Sniffington, let's go have some fun." My conversation with Dom was the last thing I remember before I woke up naked on Raya's couch. Somehow, Vlad from BB ended up on the other couch with a blowup doll firmly attached to his phallus. What the fuck did we get into last night?

# Raving with the Martians of Morgan street

"Raaaaayyyyaaaa! What the fuck went on last night bitch?" "Oh my gawd, you seriously don't remember a thing Sniffy? We got absolutely shitfaced from tequila and absinthe. We met up with Vlad and he plowed the shit out of me, the sexy Rusky stud! Then we did like a gram of cheech each, and then... well let's just say, you're not a virgin anymore kiddo." "What do ya mean I'm not a virgin anymore?" "Wow, you seriously don't remember fucking your twin hipster in the ass?" "WHAT?!?! Are you fucking serious Ray?" "Well, yeah, you seemed to enjoy it. I know Vlad and I did. I knew you were a butt pirate Sniffy. You're not Morrissey, you're, well, ok yeah, you're pretty much Morrissey." "Eh, whatever, no big whoop, if I can't recall it, that means it never happened. It's my perception over your narration, love!" "Wow, you are a spastic weirdo!" "Anyway, what's the 411 for tonight? I'm itching for a night out that I could actually remember." "That will be accomplished tonight, we're going to one of Smilez' famous treasure map raves." "Awesome! What's a treasure map rave though?" "Basically, it's a secret outlaw rave where only a handful of cool, experienced partiers are invited to, ya know, to keep the joint from getting raided and shit." "Awesome, I really can't wait. Hey, can ya please hand me the alka-seltzer please, my head feels as though my brain cells had an end of the world orgy." "Ha, sure here ya go, and remember, before we go out tonight your eating at least 3 bananas and drinking a bottle of water." "Why?" "Ha ha, you really are an adorable noob, Sniffy." After sleeping for a good eleven hours, I took an hour and a half to look like I don't care how I look, naturally. Don't judge me, it's my style! Raya looked nonchalant and gorgeous as always. The trip to our destination was marked by tricky hidden subtleties that threw off the uninvited. After the fourth clue, a green smiley face with the mouth forming an arrow pointing east, I started to get irritated. "Come down Sniffy, it ain't the destination, it's the journey, 'cause we all know the destination is the end of us all." "Yeah, yeah, I know, but these damn Vans are just so uncomfortable, I'm starting to get blisters." "You are one hell of a diva, Sniffy." "Shut up ho! Are we there yet?" "Are we there yet? Are we there yet? You're like my five year old sister, yeah we're here. There's the final clue." We knew we had reached the party. Smilez was one fuck of an eccentric character. The first four clues were basically undetectable scribbles on buildings; the final one was this gigantic neon luminescent ENTER sign. I guess he abided by the whole "they won't suspect me in the most obvious scenario" philosophy. The dude had balls no one could take that away from him, I will say that. As we enter the premises, we meld with the sea of dilated corneas, like salt dissolving in water. "Here Sniffy, pop this." "Let me guess. Roxy music is playing. I'm about to find out love is the drug, eh?" "In 45 minutes, love will overtake ya Sniffy." Sure as fuck, the dame had called it down to the second. 45 minutes on the dot later, my mind, spirit, and body were in some utopian paradise. "Are ya some kind of Auger there Raya?" "Nope, I'm just an experienced MDMA connoisseur." Everything was perfect. I had taken ecstasy before, but nothing compared to the strength and purity of what Raya had given me. "Hey Raya, give me some of that paint of yours, I have to write something on your back, ya know repay you after you wrote those words of wisdom on mine." "Ok, here ya go Sniffy." I wasn't sure what I was writing. I was simply going with the flow. After everything was said and done, about an hour later, Raya's back looked like the Rosetta stone. What I had written surprised even the egomaniacal me: when my time comes, I will gently bow before the setting sun. My eyes will shed one final tear onto God's verdant empire. Every scratch and scar on my frail carcass will tell its own story. If we go off into the abyss without anecdotes to tell, we fail in this realm. No burdens, no discontent, and no malice shall accompany me on the next leg of my predetermined quest. I will exit this perception the same way I entered it- naked, pure, and serene. My eyes will glisten from the perpendicular rays of the sun. There is a hint of jaundice, a glassy overflow, and the gaze of a man who has seen too little to conspire against himself. My heart will beat one final righteous snare, as if to say the curtain's closing kiddo, no encore this time. The sun will finally immerse itself within the horizon, waving to me one final time with a glorious flare. As it eclipses with the mountains, I close my eyes. After I force my eyelids to open, I will be in the arms of all my loved ones. Lucidity, content, and bliss are finally present for the first time. "Jeez, Sniffy, that is the most gorgeous thing I have ever heard, thank you so much for sharing that with me. I don't think I'll be showering for a month, I want to show this to everyone I know." "You're welcome love, I feel as though we are kindred spirits. You must also feel this unfathomable energy between us." "Sniffy,

I felt that energy from the first moment I offered you to suck my tits. We are fucking soul mates!" "Yeah, I think we are. Hey. Raya, I think I'm ready to lose my virginity" "But you did Sniffy, to Dom, remember?" "No I don't, so it doesn't count, I told ya that already!" "Ok hun, where do ya want to do it?" "Right here on the fucking floor, in front of everyone!" "Jeez, I love ya so much Sniffy, let's do this!" As we moved in towards one another, inch by inch, the monotonous pulsating trance in the background was finally silenced. The only thing I heard at that moment was Raya's blood flowing throughout her veins and capillaries. The lights that were dancing all over the venue like a bunch of UFO's fucked up on GHB were put out. The only thing that I saw was the pitch black abyss of Raya's beautiful pupils. I saw myself dancing in that abyss, holding a swaying Raya in a flowing hazel gown. The actual fornication process had seemed to last a millennium. The penetration of my throbbing member into her supple, angelic vaginal canal was nothing short of, well, ecstasy. The minutes leading up to the ejaculation felt like eons. As my milk finally released into her chasm, I felt my eyes roll to the back of my head. Dad would've been so proud, but fuck him, I don't care what he thinks. You would have figured that our impromptu escapade would make the crowd stare in awe as if they've witnessed the second coming of Christ himself, but no one rubbernecked, they simply went on to enjoy their own manipulated realities. After seven or so hours of Shangri-la, the inevitable serotonin drop had taken place. Zombified is probably the best word that comes to mind in describing the feeling and appearance of the poor soul who experiences the after effects of MDMA. The proverbial fall from grace had taken over my being. Call me Lucifer and paint me red, I am a fallen angel. Raya wrapped me around her body and we proceeded to leave the shindig. Feet from the door, I spotted a familiar face grooving to the beat. Like Lazarus himself resurrected from the dead, there she was. It took me but a moment to make out the silhouette of Sveta's face, and the miscellaneous lesions that were mapped all about her alabaster skin. "It's better to burn out because rust never sleeps," she whispered in my ear. "Ya like Neil Young, don't ya, sweetie?" "Yeah, I like pretty much all his songs except Needle and the Damage Done." "Ironic, ain't it?" "Yeah, us junkies are a contorted gaggle of circus folks." "So what are ya doing at a place like this?" "What? Us rig monkeys can't rave? The better question is how badly are ya coming down right now? Want a hit?" "No, I'm good. I never touch the brown stuff!" "That's good. I love how ya rich preppy shits rationalize that one drug is acceptable to use just because it's less socially taboo, yet you're all about not conforming to the norm. A bunch of hypocritical bottom feeders is what ya are!" "Guess we are; say do you happen to have any percs or sticks on ya by any chance?" "Why would I? I'm already on the ultimate sedative!" "Well, it's been great seeing ya again, but I feel like Al Capone's penis during the last days of his syphilitic deterioration, so I'm gonna go home, pop a vic and try ma' best to catch some Z's" "You got it buddy, see ya around." "You too, hun. Stay alive!" I stutter my way back to my loft, pop the downer, smoke some ganja, and like a narcoleptic pass the fuck out.

# Meatpacking with the pretties On 🔔 . ⚓ 1 2

I'm dead asleep when my ringtone rudely wakes me the fuck up. "Yo motherfucker, where the fuck are ya? Get your ass over here. NOW!" Apparently, I had totally forgotten that I was supposed to meet Dom. He was taking me to the modeling agency that he worked for. Shit man, my bad. Yo, I'll be there in twenty." "Yo dude, I know it's called fashionably late, but the pun doesn't apply to the actual business, get here ASAP!" I put on my skinny jeans and ran like Forrest Gump to the L. For the first time in my life, I got somewhere faster then it took me to take a dump. As I got to the agency Dom was huffing and puffing in front of the building. "What the hell man? You're making me look really bad here. I stuck my neck out to get you this casting call. And weren't ya supposed to wear the same outfit as me? Remember, we were gonna do the whole twins shtick." "Fuck me man, I'm way sorry. I'm still crashing from last night." "Whatever, we'll figure something out." Dom escorted me into the extravagantly chic lobby. I was greeted with a series of disapproving looks from the local modeling glitterati. "Who the fuck is this kid?" asked some 5'4" Valentino donning über-fem. "He's with me, Paolo, don't worry," Dom quickly responded. I swear if it wasn't for the fact that I was going to be a model, I would hate these arrogant twats with a passion. This is probably going to sound ludicrous, but I believe models are today's quintessential martyrs. They most defiantly are a gaggle of narcissistic simpletons with the cranial brows of simian apes, but say what you will about them they will fight to the end truly believing that they are blessed gifts from God. Isn't blind faith the most powerful defense mechanism we as human beings possess? If we truly believe something to be legitimate, no one can sway our minds from believing so. If we truly believe, we then convince ourselves that we understand. If we fathom, we perceive. If we perceive, we exist! So after a good two hours of stripping for this glassy-eyed crowd of self-deprecating socialites, decision time was upon us. Am I a model or simply another okay looking face from New England? "Congratulations, young man. Welcome to the big leagues." "Ya thanks, coach," I wanted to tell him, "but ya better use a pinch-hitter." All jokes aside, I was quite enamored about this. My dad is going to be thrilled that I'm doing something with my life. Then again, I couldn't give two flying fucks what that misanthropic boozehound had to say. "Yo, thanks for the hookup Dom, ya seriously did me a solid dude." "No sweat, hot stuff, ya owe me one motherfucker!" "Let's go out tonight. I'm buying for ya the whole night." "Okay man, sounds like a plan. I will see ya 11p.m SHARP on the Lower East Side. Here's the address of the bar. Seriously dude, this late thing you're becoming accustomed to is becoming a little passé." Dom and I hugged and we were on our way back to our respective neighborhoods, me back to my hipster-infested W'Burg and Dom back to Gay-ville, I mean, Chelsea.

# The Outer Borough

My rendezvous with Dom and the fashion glitterati pleasantly left a good taste in my mouth. The only logical thing to do was exacerbate that good taste and go out and get blitzed. I got in a few good hours of naptime in before Raya came scurrying in through my door. "Wake the fuck up Sniffy, we're going to Pluto." "Pardon? Where the hell is Pluto?" "Ha ha noob, Pluto is what we New Yorkers call Staten Island." "Oh yeah, why is that, love?" "Because it's dark, cold, and way out of the fucking way!" "Oh, that's actually pretty cheeky. So what's on Pluto then?" "Well, one thing Pluto is great for is sick house parties and collecting a nice array of illicit substances." "Hmm, that sounds titilating indeed. I'm down!" "Awesome. My boy Mikey is gonna pick us up in forty. That should give ya enough time to look like you don't care what you look like right? That's what ya always say." "Yeah, ya know me way too well by now Raya." Mikey picked us up exactly 40 minutes later. Ha, I guess punctuality is a common virtue on Pluto. So, how can I begin to describe Mikey? Mikey looked as if he was on ten illegal substances simultaneously whilst casually acting as if he was sober. "Yo, I'm rolling balls ma' peeeeppppsss," were the first words Mr. Mikey said to me, followed by an elaborate onslaught of Staten Island slang, during most of which I had sincerely no idea what the fuck he was talking about. Mikey's general lexicon consisted of the words yo, bro, kid, and a myriad of druggie lingo. "I got us some sweet 'cid, kid. We're gonna be tripping for days, bro" was an example of his grasp on the English language. Mikey's car was a 2004 Silver Nissan Altima with tinted windows of course, and his custom license plate spelled out CMYNUTZ. These plutonian folks were pretty funny if ya thought about it. "Buckle up kiddies, Uncle Mikey drives pretty fast," he warned us. Sure as hell, the bloke made me buckle up, and I was sitting in the back seat. "Dude, maybe ya should slow down. This noob Sniffy is gonna piss himself," Raya yelled out. "Fuck you, bitch! I ain't scared of shit!" "Yeah you are Sniffy, I heard ya scream when ya stepped into that dog turd." "Ok, ya got me there ha ha." Mikey's driving was indeed startling. I tried my best to act stoic but my frightened mannerisms were all too obvious. The dude went 85 fucking miles on the Verrazano Bridge entry ramp. I seriously thought that his fucking Altima was going to flip like eight times! It took us only twelve minutes to get from point A which was my pad in WB to B, Mikey's "crib" on Bloomingdale Road. The twelve minutes felt like twelve years and truth be told, his driving was responsible for me urinating in my skinny jeans; just a tad though. It is funny how every house in Staten Island looks as though it had budded off another house with the exact same dimensions and colors. His house was about eleven different levels, each level being only about five feet up from the previous. His house was pretty much like a game of half-played Jenga. As soon as we entered his abode, we were presented with two or so grams of fine looking Colombian powder, already cut up on his living room coffee table. To my fancy the cocaine was extremely pure and potent. It had a natural pinkish hue to it, which meant it was legit. Merely one line and one freeze had completely numbed my gums and septum. "This shit is top of the line kiddies. Only uncle Mikey has connections this nice." The dude wasn't kidding, this shit was no joke. It took me a minute to realize it, but the cheeky fucker had spelled out "Uncle Mikey" with the cocaine. Line after line quickly disappeared. After thirty minutes, "Uncle Mikey" was simply uncle. Twenty minutes after that, only 'u' and half of a 'c' were left. "Three rails left fo' my peeps yo," Mikey told us. "One for uncle Mikey, one for ma' girl Rayray, and one fo' my new boy, lawd Sniffs." Mikey snorted his line like an Orec. I railed my share and started to twitch a bit, but nothing too serious. I was used to being on the precipice of an overdose. Raya was already in pretty bad shape, she had insufflated as much as the boys, which was probably not a great idea on her behalf. "C'mon Rayray ya got this girl," Mikey said. Like a true trooper, Raya garnered her remaining strength and took the final bumps. "You okay hun?" I asked her. "No, actually, I have to go lie down. My heart feels a little funny, Sniff." As soon as she had uttered that sentence, Mikey ran up to his room and brought down a little blue bottle with "XX" written on it in permanent black marker. "Open yo mouth Rayray. Dr. Uncle Mikey is gonna make ya feel legit!" Raya seemed to really trust this maniac and did what he had asked. Mikey measured out five drops and dripped them one by one into her throat. "Arrghhh!!!! This shit is disgusting! What the fuck is this, Mikey?" "It's high grade liquid Xanax, girl, it's gonna balance ya out perfectly." After about a minute and a half it seemed as though the sociopath was right. The shit he had given Raya seemed to help her out. The only uncomfortable thing was witnessing Raya battle the negative effects of her quasi-speedball. Every time she dozed off for a moment, she quickly woke up as if having one of those sweat-drenching nightmares. After pseudo-seizing for a bit, she dozed off to sleep. "Ya two better spend the night here. I'll drive ya goons back to BK first thing tomorrow. Nighty night playa, it's been Uncle Mikey's esteemed pleasure to party with ya." "Yo, the feeling is mutual ma' brother." "Ha ha, you're starting to talk like one of us Staten Islanders, guess you really are becoming one of us. Hold on, I see you're a pimp, I'm gonna get us something that will really blow ya mind, Sniff." Uncle Mikey went back up to his room and came back with what seemed like a baggie filled with Meth. "Yo, we're doing meth dude? I don't think it's such a good idea, we're already tweaking like fuck from the cheech." "Wow! Ya really are a noob aren't ya kid? This is true blue Newark Dima" "Dima?!? I honestly don't know what that is dude." "It's DMT. You're gonna dig it my man, trust me." Mikey packed some of the DMT into a glass pipe and told me to take three of the deepest pulls I could. He told me that it would burn and sting my lungs but the effects were WELL worth the discomfort. You know the saying: when on Pluto do as the Plutonians do! The three pulls were indeed borderline unbearable. Each pull was worse and worse than the one before it. By the third pull, the hallucinations were indescribably overwhelming. My world had become an active kaleidoscope! Every piece of furniture, every knick-knack in Mikey's house had begun to communicate with me. I felt the essence of everything, everyone, and most importantly of myself. Unlike LSD or magic mushrooms, synesthesia was not prevalent. The five senses I knew were instead replaced with five different senses unfathomable to the coherent mind. The best way I could describe my experience was controlled schizophrenia. It's as I knew everything was off, askew, but I could control this delectable perception. At one point, I had realized that I was turning into a Ferris wheel, quickly changing my form into other contorted infrastructure: I was a building, I was a ship, I was a bridge. The trip was un-fucking-believable. The only problem was that it was way too short for my liking, maybe fifteen minutes altogether. As quickly as the trip had begun was exactly how fast it ended. The hallucinations ceased. At that moment, the only thing I could focus on was Mikey's Cheshire cat grin. "Pretty fucking awesome, eh ma' dude?" "Dude! That was, that was, that was..." "I know, my dude, ya welcome." Mikey took me to the basement, where I would crash the night, or what was at this point the morning. He checked up on Raya one final time, and was satisfied with her condition. I sublimely passed out with a smile on my face and I woke up with a smile. It was 3:45 PM. I went up to the kitchen area and was greeted by "Hello!" from Mikey and Raya. "Want some bacon and eggs ma' dude?" Mikey hospitably offered. "Oh, I'm good man. I got a model shoot coming up. Oh my goodness! As soon as I uttered that sentence, I realized that I was supposed to meet up with Dom last night at some bar. FUCK MY LIFE!!!

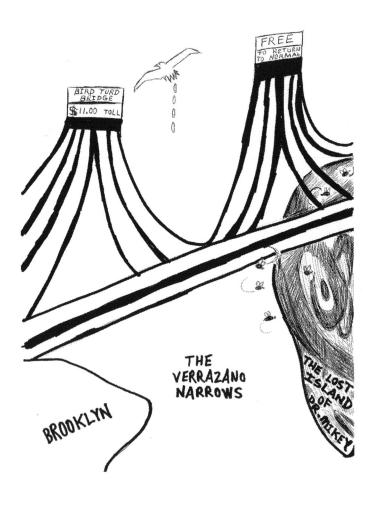

# The ferry, the subterranean way

I still can't believe I didn't meet up with Dom! Even though I was still lightheaded from my encounters on Pluto, I asked Mikey to give me a ride to the Staten Island ferry so I could go to Chelsea and apologize to Dom face to face. Mikey was hesitant due to the fact he was still crashing profusely, but eventually agreed. The ride to Manhattan on the ferry was just what my stamina needed. My body and mind were battered and disheveled but the cool Hudson air felt quite convalescing. I got off the ferry and took the first taxi I could hail straight to Dom's place. Dom lived in a very luxurious building. This place was no joke, I thought. If this cat is making enough to live in this multi-million dollar pad from modeling, imagine what I could make. I tried giving Dom a ring to tell him I was by his building but before I got the chance to dial him he had stepped out of the lobby. "DOM!!" I yelled. He turned around, looking hurt. "You suck dude! I can't stand flakes. Take care, man." "Dude, I'm so sorry. I was fucked up last night and totally forgot. Is there anything I can do to make it up to ya?" "Yeah, go away for now. I'm not in the mood. I'll call ya later if anything." I felt like a piece of shit! Not only did I completely jeopardize my career and hurt a really nice dude who had stuck his neck out for me, but I also felt the effects from last night's partying. I only had $14 on me so I couldn't get a cab straight into WB. My dad's money wasn't coming in for another two days! Eh, I was in NYC, so I figured might as well take the train. My father had warned me against ever taking public transportation in NYC but I had taken it a few times already with Raya and it wasn't bad at all. I walked a few blocks, down to Union square and caught the L. Now for all of you who have never taken the NYC subway before here's a little experiment you can do when you eventually do get to ride one. Go on the subway, any line will do, and put on your headphones while playing the music at full blast. Observe in a blasé New Yorker way and I guarantee you will spot the ten characters I'm going to list, some of whom might qualify as endangered species on the Discovery channel. This has been written with helpful suggestions that will aid in your voyeuristic tendencies!

1   The pan handling aspiring musician: this cat probably has talent, probably had his opportunity and probably had money, but blew it all on drugs and dug his hole too deep to ever scurry out of. They will tell you something along the lines of: "Hey guys, I need to feed my kids, so any contributions would be great." in reality the only thing that they've got to feed is their insatiable appetite for Afghani Blue. This is best observed while listening to Alternative 90's rock.

2   The pregnant lady with five uncontrollable

kids: now, contrary to popular belief I actually like children, but witnessing the hell-spawned progeny conceived by this horrid baby factory makes even the most notorious Megan's list pedophile detest children. Shit, even the Catholic Church would be hesitant with these little gnats as altar boys. The mom is busy chatting up on her cell phone and stuffing her face with pork rinds and cheesecake while her unbearable abortions-gone-wrong torment the subway locale. Crying, yelling and farting; simply put that's all you get from them. The MP3 player is officially the greatest invention since sliced bread. I'm fairly certain that if I would have to take NYC transit on a regular basis without the aid of my music, well, Sylvia Plath, you could eat your heart out. This is best observed while listening to Techno.

3   At least three loud and obnoxious adolescents: so, not only must the regular straphangers put up with little shit stains who don't know any better, but they must also turn the other cheek to hormone spewing teenagers. In my opinion, the teens are the worst of the worst. They're old enough to understand how to act but still choose to belt out profanities, blast their shitty contemporary smut-laden music, and sometimes even get physical. This is best observed listening to classical music.

4   The scared tourist: truth be told, the chances are high that you are going to be this character. They are constantly checking the train map,

asking everyone where their stop is, scurrying back and forth between train cars, and not making eye contact with anyone. Simply put, every non-new Yorker must go through this process. It greatly helps if you know someone in NYC to show you the ropes, but if you don't, you'll be somewhat startled. You're going to try your hardest to decipher through the static what the conductor moans over the intercom. To no avail, you ask someone where so-and-so is, and if they're nice they'll tell you honestly but if they are an asshole, which they probably will be, you're going to end up somewhere deep in NYC where nobody looks or speaks like you. Good luck buddy! This is best observed listening to heavy metal.

5   The morbidly obese man taking up 2 to 3 seats: this individual is one of God's abstract art exhibits. It's as if God pondered "how can I make a modern Goliath?" The only problem was that the centrifuge the lord used to conjure up said man-beast went haywire and height got replaced with girth. My Rusky buds from BB often have bets on whether this leviathan will be able to stand up when his stop comes up. He usually starts getting ready to attempt to stand three or four stops before his own. If gravity prevails, he leans against the doors, praying for his stop to come as quickly as possible. Occasionally, balance is lost and he flops to the floor grunting a glorious profanity, but somehow always makes it back home. What

a trooper. This is best observed listening to anything with a tuba.

6  The Wino: truly ethereal in every way is the subway Wino, usually with urine stained gym shorts, whiskey-infused facial hair, and a magnificent mane fully loaded with lice. Quite exceptional in adapting to society, thinking all the while that he can trick enforcement officials by pouring amber colored whiskey into transparent spring water bottles. The Wino will not bother you if you don't bother him. Give him a pat on the head; he will be grateful. This is best observed listening to Opera.

7  The Schizophrenic: pretty well educated is the subway schizophrenic. This bloke usually preaches some religious insight, most of which is from the book of revelations. "The end is coming, repent your sins before the second coming!" You kind of have to appreciate his stamina he will preach and preach and preach. Usually said schizophrenic is accompanied by a poster board with a biblical verse or two. This is best observed listening to adult contemporary.

8  The Puritan: still thinking that civilization revolves around ethics and human decency, the puritan sits isolated in the corner judging the subway masses. No one is good enough and everyone to her is simply a hell-bound sinning fear-monger. Though rarely voicing out her opinions, her facial tics and contortions lay out the foundation of her true beliefs. Yet

she still refuses to move out of Sodom, I mean NYC, and move to somewhere that she would find truly hunky-dory, like Idaho. This is best observed listening to Grunge.

9   "The Freak": Believe me you'll just know, and they will be what you're listening to.

10   The only other sane individual on the train that gives you a discreet nod as if telling you "I know dude, I know."

# Holy shit Dom! The First nexus Limbo: Hell/ Downtown

I was elated for successfully taking the train back home without getting lost or stabbed. The unfortunate thing was that I lost service on my cell phone heading back so I missed three phone calls and two texts from Dom. "Ok, I forgive yo punk ass, Sniff. Now, get your twin ass back to Union Square. Let's get some caffeine in us and chat." I jetted to the train in order to get there as soon as I could. I got back to Union Square and met up with Dom. "This is where I go to observe humanity, Sniff. It might seem that there is nothing here, but this is the supreme nexus of heaven and hell." "What do ya mean, D?" "Just sit back and watch the show. I mean after all, humanity is one big act. We insignificant humans scurry around, aimlessly craving only to understand. There is this impossible notion of understanding. I came to terms with the fact that we know nothing. Many great figures throughout history, from Socrates to Nietzsche, have admitted that they know absolutely nothing. I used to do a lot of drugs myself, Sniff. During one of my horrid

MDMA crashes, I had an epiphany that would change my life forever." "What was it, dude?" "I just shut my eyes and saw myself as a microscopic bacterium, floating with millions if not billions of other bacteria. We were all in the digestive tract of some greater being and our function was to help this exalted being exist. The next day, I was on the N train, passing over the Manhattan Bridge; I gazed through the window, and everyone, everything down below me looked like the same bacteria I had imagined myself to be the night before. I thought to myself for a moment, isn't everyone God in a way?" "How so, dude?" "Well just picture it, each one of us has these billions of organisms in us, so we're kind of like its world and they are our inhabitants. If we die, they die! And if Earth gets blown up from a nuclear war or meteor or something, there is absolutely nothing we can do. Fate and faith are both perceptions; everything is a perception. Dreams, lucidity, dementia, pessimism, optimism, life, death, everything dude! Milton said it best when he said that the mind is the only object powerful enough to turn heaven into hell or hell into heaven. I might be paraphrasing, but you get the gist. So if we align ourselves to not commit in understanding anything, we succeed. We'll never know anything dude! The infinite, other dimensions, the universe, it's all out of our grasp. As long as we admit that we can't fathom it, what we truly need to understand will be presented to us, and if it isn't, we'll rationalize our minds to the point where believe that it was meant to be." "Holy Shit D, ya seriously are fucking blowing my mind!" "Just shut ya mouth kid, and watch. This is the proverbial melting pot we learned about in grade school, but the liquid in this said pot is significantly more viscous then advertised." "What am I supposed to see D?" "That I can't tell ya bro, but you'll sure as fuck will know it." I swear, it must have taken less than three minutes for me to spot what Dom had wanted me to witness. The majority of people walking by us in Union Square looked more or less normal. Some were bohemian, some were flamboyant, and some seemed downright leprous, but one in particular caught my eye the instant I spotted her. I have never encountered anything like what I saw. This had to be some joke that Satan was playing on us! This woman, if you can call it that, was a 4'5" Albino, with dreadlocks and booty shorts. She was rollerblading whilst simultaneously walking her miniature pinscher. Before I could even utter a sound, Dom's gaze had met mine. "The nexus, dude. Welcome to the threshold of all that is delectably asinine." "Dude I seriously didn't know these creatures had existed." "Nah kid, not only didn't ya know such creatures existed, but you don't know jack squat! Anything is possible, everything is real and nothing is classified!" Few minutes passed and I was still pretty flabbergasted from witnessing that THING. Unexpectedly, I was barraged by two more specimens. The first creature seemed normal when I first saw him. Oh it's just a punk on a skateboard, with a normal build; aesthetically pleasing, pretty normal all together until he turned his head. I gasped in awe, something that I absolutely never do! This poor kid was missing a good third of his head and face. "Craniotomy, I think it's called. I could be wrong though, I'm a model, not a Doctor damn it," Dom told me. This unfortunate lad! He could not have been more than sixteen but already life decided to teach him a hell of a lesson. As soon as I thought that to myself, I was reminded of the excerpts I had written on Raya's back during our MDMA experience. Every scratch and scar on my frail carcass will tell its own story. If we go off into the abyss without anecdotes to tell, we fail in this realm. Well, if that was the case this kid had an epic poem the likes of the Odyssey or Iliad to share with the people on the other side. Moments after the kid left, I witnessed something that

I couldn't quite stomach. I could not believe that this was possible. Now, I have seen Siamese twins many times on television but never in person, and certainly nowhere near this mess. Two human girls were attached at the head, barely able to walk and continuously viewed as a sideshow. "How could anyone live like that?" "They're not as miserable as ya think, dude." "What?!?! How could ya say that?" "Get off of your fantastic high horse and feel some compassion, ya turd! What I'm about to tell you is something that will be paramount in you discovering content. Keep this in your back pocket the same way I do. A few years back, I was the most miserable wretch that had ever floated in this world. I convinced myself that I was the devil, the bearer of woe, the antichrist! On the verge of downing 500 milligrams of Oxycontin, my best friend barged in and tackled me to the ground. After a stint in the nearest psych ward, my best friend and savior gave me a plane ticket. 'Your plane leaves in two hours, either get on it or fuck off,' he told me. I had no idea where the hell I was going. Only when I had gotten to JFK airport did I realize that he had bought me a ticket to northern Finland. Inside the itinerary packet, there was a post-it note with the words BRIGHT NIGHT written on it. As soon as I got my luggage, I saw a large Scandinavian holding a sign with BRIGHT NIGHT written on it. 'You must be Dom,' he asked pleasantly. Well, long story short he took me to a hut and made me consume some sort of psychedelic concoction. I still have no fucking idea what was in that brew. Two hours after consumption, he took me outside, stripped me naked, and laid me in the snow; I was unexpectedly warm. As I gazed up into the sky the lovely northern lights were pleasantly dancing all over. I was in heaven at that moment. A few incalculable moments later, my spirit animal appeared to me, a black ram. It told me to stop idolizing this whole yin-yang/stasis/balance hoopla.

The world consists of a natural good and a natural evil, to balance itself out. I was to concentrate on being neutral, an everyman if you will. I was to be smack dab between the septum of the spectrum, not in the black or white areas. So, Sniffs, the moral of this tangent is, just don't believe in this karma hype. Don't do anything to anyone unless you truly believe you have to. Things always fall into place dude. Unfortunately, sometimes they fall in unpleasing patterns, but with a little acceptance and mind over matter, the shapes can be re-shaped into more opalescent designs. The three individuals you saw only seem damned from the get-go. Hell, maybe they are. But my guess is that what they lack in physical benevolence they make up in mental and spiritual harmony. Never, ever let ill-fated battles beat you in existential warfare!"

# The Other nexus-purgatory/ Heaven-in the heights

Dom had opened up a part of my being that had been dormant up to this point and time. "Now that you've witnessed the unfair, I'm gonna show ya that humanity still has a few proper traits left in it." Though Dom was only four years older than me, I felt as if he'd seen the entire world and that all I witnessed was an iota of my own perception. Continuing onward, we hopped on the A line and went to the northernmost part of Manhattan. The Washington Heights/Inwood region of NYC felt right as soon as we got off the train. It had this indescribably pleasant ambiance to it. "This is the positive nexus, Sniffy. The antithesis of what you've just witnessed in Union Square." WaHI was a collaboration of every demographic I could think of. Instead of animosity, acceptance was prevalent amongst the locals. It felt right! Union Square was also representative of the proverbial melting pot but consisted of, as far as I had seen it, malignancy and strife. The neighborhood mixed all of its ingredients gracefully. People here marched to the beat of their own drum, but made sure to carve out a path to suffice everyone's needs. It was a linear realm, not a fucking labyrinth. "Just like Union Square Sniff, sit down here and observe. Really just let existence show ya what it has evolved into." Dom and I had sat down on a bench overlooking St. Nicholas. The first thought that scurried throughout my head was that no tourist would ever come up here. Not only are the Heights too far from their overpriced, trademarked, franchise owned, décor-laden restaurants from Times Square, but it is also moments away from the Bronx. No tourist would come within three miles of the Bronx. Like Union Square, the first character I noticed was a very short woman, maybe 4'8" or so if I had to guess. The little woman I had seen in Union made my heart cringe; this one, however, had a certain profound mystique about her. Instead of waddling like the previous one, this one glided. There was this unmistakable aura surrounding her. She stopped by us and asked Dom for a lighter. Her voice was eloquent and passionate. If I had closed my eyes and simply heard her speak, I would have imagined that the sound was belting out of a six-foot tall operatic Soprano, not a petite morsel. Dom gave her a light and she thanked him. This gal was nothing short of sensual. She was, despite her height, a heartbreaker. As if Dom had conversed with God almighty himself and had initiated a cosmic juxtaposition, the second encounter in the Heights was surreal. A teenage kid rolled by us on his skateboard, as one had in Union. I expected to see this teen turn around and show some horrendous physical deformation, but he seemed perfectly fine. His skateboarding skills were incredible. He railed and ollied and grinded and whatever other slang these potheads used, perfectly. Clearly he was a master at his craft. The thing that really melted my cynical heart was his interaction with his kid brother. The little guy was clearly just learning the ropes of how to skateboard. He was tagging a few feet behind his big bro. Though big bro could've easily just skated ahead and met up with other esteemed boarders, he was spending time teaching his little brother how to skateboard properly. When his sibling fell and scraped his knee, the older brother ditched his board and ran to the aid of the little one. The simple act of throwing the board away was enough to bring a warm feeling that reverberated throughout my being. He threw away what he was good at, what made him happy, and what was most certainly his identity to check up on his family. I really don't think I would ever do that! I had totally forgotten that the "family first" mantra still existed in NYC, but these two had totally rekindled that notion for me. "So, I have seen both a little person and an adolescent on a skateboard. Let me guess Dom, I'm about to see me some Siamese twins, eh?" "Eh, I don't know Sniff, what's that look like yonder?" I turned my head and was ready to see another pair of grotesque conjoined twins. Instead, I saw triplets. Three darling little girls, maybe six or seven years old were skipping along, all holding hands. I hate to admit it, but this sight had actually brought a tear to my eye. "I have never seen anything so fucking pure in my entire life, Dom" "Oh it exists dude; ya just have to focus on it." The three little angels were followed by their parents. Like the girls, their folks were also holding hands. The sun cast a shimmering ray upon the family, as if trying to portray just how graceful and immaculate God really was. I felt like a new man. I have no bloody idea how Dom had assembled this chain of events, but truth be told I couldn't really give a shit. The gist was that I had now been converted from a societal cynic into a societal darling. "Thanks Dom. I doubted ya bud, but wow man, I don't think I can thank ya enough" "Don't thank me yet dude. I have simply shown you that both good and bad are prevalent everywhere you look. The way you shape and

perceive your life is completely in the hands of the beholder."
I had a new lease on life. I didn't care that I sounded like
one of those depression medication commercials. I was truly
content for the first time since, well, ever. "Now that your
mind is at least halfway out of the gutter, take this." Dom
had given me a business card from the modeling agency he
was part of with a date and time on it. "9:30 AM Thursday,
be there or seriously fuck off this time!" Those were the
exact words written on it. "I have to go run a few errands
around here kiddo. Ya think you'll be able to make it back
to hipsterville in one piece?" "Oh yeah, I'm a regular train
guru by now. Thanks again for everything dude, I'll see ya
Thursday."

# some Cø ime in søℋø/ TriBeca, I gøt a clip før ya bitch !

I got to the agency at 8:30 am, an hour before Dom had requested. "I can't believe my fucking eyes, Sniff. You're early, and I think it's time for Belphegor to get out his Sable fur coat from storage." "Yeah, ya taught me a thing or two that day bro. I'm gonna change the way I do things from now on." "Good man. So here's the deal. We're going to finally be doing that twins shoot. It's gonna be huge dude. A lot of heads are intrigued by this concept." This time the glitterati seemed to have a different perception of me. Instead of witnessing their smug disapproval of my being there, now they greeted me like one of their own. "Would you care for some sparkling water sir?" one of the agents asked. I had quite a different experience this time. Dom and I got escorted to a back dressing room to be fitted in our costumes. I must say that even my skinny jean wearing ass felt tight in the garb they donned us in. I seriously had to adjust my breathing accordingly to not burst one of the seams on the suit they put me in. Dom was fashioned first and seemed flawlessly natural. I actually squealed like a pig runt for the first few minutes whilst getting acclimated to having my intestines contorted by the tightness. The suits they put on us were indeed magnanimous. They were fairly flamboyant in their appearance, but hey, isn't all upper echelon clothing? Dom and I looked like gay matadors. Then again, all matadors pretty much look gay if ya think about it. Our pants were shin low and left very little to the imagination. The top of our costume had more glitter on it then a stripper's asshole. They even made us wear matching tiny fezzes. "Welcome to the big leagues kiddo," Dom told me, "could've sworn I heard that before. This is déjà vu all over again, right Yogi?" The actual shoot went off without a hitch. "You look like you've been doing this for years," one of the photographers told me. A general appeasement was prevalent throughout the crowd. I had found what I was good at, something I could tell Dad and my cunt step-mom. After a few hours of miscellaneous posing and contortion, we were finished. It felt incredible to actually get out of those clothes. "Here you go kid, great job! You earned it. We'll be calling you again very shortly, you can count on that." The agent handed me an envelope with a check inside, consisting of $2,500. Wow! Not bad for a good for nothing apathetic druggie. I felt like Adonis. Hopefully narcissism wouldn't take over. I'm sure I can control the high life. To celebrate my newfound status, Dom took me to a few swanky SoHo bars. The bars were all exuberant in every way imaginable. The crowd consisted of the who's who of Manhattan society. Ritzy Amazonian models, both male and female, promenaded around the bar, consistently comparing themselves to one another. 6'1" Sapphic goddesses adorned the lounge area looking for millionaire boy-toys to support their luxurious lusts. The guys were nothing short of "pretty" themselves, androgynous as they were. Dom and I fit in swimmingly. "Four shots of

SoCo lime for me and my twin," Dom told the gorgeous bartender. "No prob, that'll be $88 sir." $88 for four tiny shots would cost someone $3 to concoct in their own abode, but hey it's all about the environment right? As I glanced around the establishment, a weird thought scurried throughout my mind. I, at that point, truly wished that I was impotent. As masochistic and deranged as that might sound, I had convinced myself that impotence would lead me to a higher spiritual realm. I mean, think about it: Buddhist and Thessalonian monks are abstinent and they are light years more insightful then your run of the mill sexual deviants. Sex was nothing more than an addiction and I of all people knew the repercussions of being committed to certain ritualistic rights. Drugs and alcohol had been a nuisance for me since I could remember. I always refrained from sex, aside from the handful of times in NYC because my rational philosophy led to me being somewhat content. Not only did it give my body, mind, and soul time to rejuvenate after the pummeling of illicit substances that I had and would put into it, but it made me original, separated me from this flock of vice laden, cum-swilling fashionistas. After nine or so more overpriced shots of otherwise cheap alcoholic swill, Dom took me to a quiet corner couch and told me something I had never expected to hear from him. "So basically Sniff, here's the deal. The agency is enamored with you and everything, but you seriously have to lose at least eight pounds before our next gala." "Pardon me dude, but what the fuck? I'm already technically anorexic for my height and weight proportion. Why on God's green earth do I have to lose even more weight?" "Just trust me dude, take this. It'll be your best friend, much cleaner and less dangerous than that cocaine you fancy." "What the hell is this, dude? Didn't ya preach to me how my mind is the only thing necessary for me to find enlightenment? Now ya give me speed!?" "It's not really speed dude, it's more like a focus pill. Be optimistic. I've been taking this A.D.D medication since the sixth grade and it has brought nothing but positive results for me and everyone else who I gave it to." "Dude, seriously, I'm already hooked on like seven other things. Do ya thing adding another vice to my already hefty repertoire is a good idea? I swear to God dude if ya are responsible for me kicking the bucket, I'll come get ya! But alright, ya do know the ins and outs of this game substantially better than I do, so I'll take your word for it." "Great! Take them and shed those few pounds. The next place we're going to next week will leave you breathless." I got home having mixed feelings about Dom, this career, and the speed he had given me. I've tried it before and honestly liked it too much, so getting hooked on it was basically inevitable. I started out low with 40 milligrams and waited to see if I could restrain myself from taking more. Close to an hour later, I took another 120 milligrams. Within the next four days the bottle had seemingly evaporated. The only positive thing that came from me being constantly tweaked out was that I managed to complete the majority of housework that had been accumulating for some time. Dishes got washed, laundry done, loft cleaned, and other otherwise procrastinated tasks were finally finished. I was so spun the last four days that I had lost eleven pounds instead of eight. That would make the glitterati euphoric, but the repercussions from the meds were evident. Both physically and mentally my being was rejecting them. Physically, I had developed severe ulcers from not eating. Though I had not went to a physician, the searing abdominal pain and coughing up of bloody mucus was a diagnosis any cretin could plainly see. Mentally, I had begun to experience what was known as "amphetamine psychosis," where everything was distorted to the point that I was completely convinced that schizophrenia had a firm, permanent grasp on my being. The crash couldn't come quickly enough. I really needed sleep and judging from my body and mind failing it was coming up relatively fast. I passed out whilst going to the bathroom for the first time in God knows how long, passed the fuck out right on the toilet seat. How graceful of me. If only the models and agents could've seen this. I would have probably have slept in that scatological position for another week if Dom hadn't knocked on my door. "Sniff, you in there buddy? Is everything alright dude?" I jerked up, put on some drawers and opened the door up for Dom. "Holy comedown, batman! Wow dude, you took all the pills, didn't you?" "Yeah, but it's your own fucking fault man, ya gave them to me. That's like giving a chimpanzee some feces. Ya don't do something like that man!" "Well, look on the bright side. You lost the pounds you were supposed to drop. As for the bags under your eyes, that is nothing a little makeup can't help" "I feel like shit dude, go away so I can get some sleep. Oh, and bring me a banana or two. I need the potassium." "Nope, I ain't going anywhere without you. You're my date for the Tribeca film festival dude, and it's the hottest ticket in NYC. Get your ass dressed, I'll wait for you." "Alright, alright, I can't say no to something like that. Give me half an hour or so, dude. As Dom and I walked out of my building, I was expecting for us to catch the L train into Manhattan, but Dom had a surprise for me. "Welcome to the zenith, buddy." Outside of the building sat, a gloriously extravagant black Hummer limousine, complete with all the accoutrements that were necessary for the highlife. Inside it were five flawless models, two girls for me and three males for Dom. Somehow, my Russian buddy Vlad had managed to sneak in. Gee, I wonder what the fuck he had to do for Dom to let him com. Bottles of Cristal Rose were presented,' and to top things off a good two pounds of grayish-black

Russian Beluga caviar were inside the limousine as well. "Dude this is legit, how are ya affording all of this swag?" "It's not me paying for everything, noob, it's the agency. Keep looking good and they'll keep treating you good. The philosophy is as simple and wholesome as that." I loved watching Vladdy boy getting rejected by the models. "C'mon chickies, you know you want some of Vladdy!" "Let's have a seven-sum," one of the models offered. "Everyone but the creepy Russian dude is welcome!" "Hey, fuck you! At least I'm not a fucking Mary-Kate Olsen wannabe. I'm hotter than all of you fucks!" I would have said no, but I just didn't care at that moment. Two bottles of overpriced champagne in my system hindered my pseudo-righteous stance against sexual deviancy, and away we went into orgy land. Poor Vlad just watched from the sidelines, but at least he managed to beat one out. When we finally arrived at the festival, two models literally fell out of the limo. What an entrance! The film fest was elaborate yet contrived. All the celebrities at the gala smirked and snickered while hopeful up and comers tried their darnedest to net a connection or two. It is better to burn out because rust never sleeps. As far as I'm concerned, all these devolved vultures are rust upon human decency. These prostitutes pull out every trick out of their silk sleeves to nab notoriety. How is that any different than a common streetwalker turning tricks for smack? "Oh Mr. So-and-So, I'm your biggest fan. Hey, check out this project I'm working on…" What a bunch of degenerates. I would never whore myself out to the masses. I enjoyed being on top of the pyramid. The only problem with standing on the pinnacle is that there is nowhere to go but down. It's a very thin line one must walk to keep from plummeting down to mediocrity, or worse. I was NOT going to trip! I was in no shape to watch these bullshit films. I was on a healthy regimen of cocaine, ketamine, alcohol, marijuana, and now amphetamines. My mind started to twirl like an epileptic ballerina from watching these pompous douche bags talk about and then play their half-assed projects. "The Elixir of Independence" was the first film. Some feminist dyke-in-training had made a 26 minute film on how wine is the blood of all women or some shit like that. I loved Vlad at this point, because the Russian scamp managed to convince the cougar next to him to give him a hand job while the film was rolling. Whatever, I put up with this bullshit and I didn't care. I was on top, baby! Staring down on these simians was I. However, three or four more mindless films later and I wanted no more to do with it. "Yo, I'm taking off D. This shit is wearing me out." "Ha. Can't say I blame ya, man; see ya next week for the shoot. Stay safe bud, go and get yourself some sleep. You deserve it, man." Vlad was finished with his newly found 40-something year old cougar and decided to tag along with me. I told him that he could come with, but don't interrupt Sniff's beauty sleep. He agreed and I hailed the first cab I saw. There would be no more trains for Sniff, only limos or at the worst, taxis, from now on.

# New York Cents vs. New York Dollars

My second attempt at catching some well deserved slumber was hastily interrupted by Raya storming into my loft. "Long time no see Cokey, get yo ass up! Your aunt Rayray is taking you somewhere super special. What the hell is the Rusky doing here?" "Oh c'mon bitch, I can't go anywhere. I'm barely conscious right now; we'll just go some other time, like next year when I wake up. Take Vlad with ya." "No Sniff, we're leaving now, and definitely no Vlad, he's a fucking creep! I had to bend over backwards to score these Yankee/Mets subway series tickets. They're not just regular seats, I got us suite tickets bitch! Now get off of your semen encrusted bed and let's go!" "Only for you will I get up girl, ya better be grateful. My time is worth a lot of money these days." "Jeez Sniff; get off of your fucking high horse. I'm doing this as a solid for ya. Ya know, for actually not being a bum anymore and having a career" "I know, I'm sorry for snapping love, I'm just so out of it." "It's fine, I forgive ya, now c'mon man, we gotta catch the train if we want to make it to the stadium in time." "I'm too good for trains.

Let's take a limo, my treat." "Hey, look at ya, Mr. Superstar. But no, we're taking the train. It's called a subway series for a reason. The train is a New York staple, and we're taking it whether ya like it or not." "Ya think Vlad will be alright?" "Ah never mind. I don't care." "Now, let's go! C'MON!" The damn train took forever but when we arrived at Yankee Stadium all my surliness had fallen by the wayside. One gander at this ethereal monolith and I was hooked on being a bonafide Yankee fanatic. I had never watched or appreciated sports before, but in an instant I had found my team, and I was now officially a Yankee. The New York Yankees were quintessentially New York. They were diverse, grand, and revered. I can't say the same for the Mets. The New York Mets were kind of like the Yankees' autistic younger cousins. They tried their darnedest to compete on a yearly basis, but always fell flat on their disproportionate faces. In a way, these two teams signified all that was human, otherworldly, and surreal if you think about it. The Yankees represented euphoria and optimism, while the Mets represented melancholy and pessimism. Yankee stadium was heaven, Shangri-la, utopia while Citi Field was Hell, the inferno, Anti-Eden. Yanks were the harmony, and the Mets chaos. These two teams were the proverbial yin-yang spectrum. I told Raya that Satan probably played for the Yanks before he joined the Mets. "What does that mean, Sniff?" "Think about it. Satan is the fallen Angel. He started off playing in heaven for the Yankees, but then got traded to the hell that is the Mets. Before I entered the stadium, I proudly bought some Yankee paraphernalia: an authentic hat, a Jeter jersey, and even an official Yankee beanie-baby for Vlad. I fucking love this team! Seemingly all of New York was present at this event. Two-thirds of the stadium had Yankee apparel, the other third Mets. This comparison reminded me of the deep philosophical insight Dom had enlightened me with.

The majority of the people were Yankee fans; hence they were good in one way or another. The rest were Met fans; they were bad but were a necessity in being, for without malcontent good cannot be evaluated. What better a way to see good prevail over evil then witnessing the holy Yankees kick the shit out of the loathsome Metropolitans? This was truly great! By the third inning, the Yanks were stomping all over the Mets. What a shocker, right? The final score was 12 to 3. I was shocked that the meek Mets managed to score that many runs. The final out of the game was then quickly followed by Frank Sinatra's "New York New York". It's hard to stomach, though, given that both teams are from New York but they seemingly represent completely different aspects. Guess life isn't that much different from a baseball game. I thought of the notion of civil war. Two sides who are fighting one another are basically brethren who are quarreling over their own land. If baseball were a civil war, then the Mets would be the close-minded racist bigots of the South who want to keep things the way they are, no matter how bad things get. The Yankees are the evolved Northerners who want change for the better. No matter what happens, the North and the Yankees prevail. Everything was going my way. I was a successful, adorable male model, I had great friends and endless financial support from the family, and to top things off I was now an official New Yorker. I was a Yankee, and no one could take that away from me. I just hope Vlad didn't burn down my fucking loft.

# Tier Drop

"I'm all about being ironic but don't like admitting it. Ooh, MGMT is playing on the radio. Can I have one more PBR, por favor?" I had heard that asinine utterance at a dive bar in the Gramercy neighborhood of Manhattan. This was the first step for me detesting my fellow hipsters. Raya and I went to this cool bar after the Yankees onslaught and were not so happy to observe the hipster infestation that was going on throughout NYC. "Wow, Sniff ya know what, I thought this hipster bullshit would blow off sooner or later but it looks worse and worse every passing day." "Hey, I'm a hipster Raya. Well I'll never admit to it, but ya can say I'm a closeted hipster." "You're a closeted a lot of things, ya queer, but I think we're getting a tad too old to be participating in this charade. Maybe those close-minded inner Brooklynites have a point. Maybe this hipster thing is getting out of control!" "No way! Why should we change? We are who we are. If they have a problem with us then they can move the fuck out of New York." "That's the thing, ya retard, they are moving out! Can't ya see, we're responsible for the rent skyrocketing. We're all well off one way or another. We never admit it but you know the truth, we are a bunch of lazy bums supported by daddy and mommy. We arrive, we inflate rent, and they leave. If I was a true blue New Yorker, I would loathe us as well. Think it's about time for all of us to move out of NYC and back to New England." "You're an idiot! I'm done having this conversation." I stormed out of the bar and pondered to myself why I was such a fucking hypocrite. Hearing those hipster cunts had made me ill to my stomach, but hearing anti-hipster slander coming from Raya made me even angrier. I don't know who the fuck I am, man. I looked at my cell and realized my dad has seemingly been trying to contact me for a few days. CALL ME NOW SON! The texts took over my inbox. I built up the intestinal fortitude to give pops a ring, and to my chagrin he was far from being angry. "Hey buddy, I heard you're a model now. I guess the old man was too naive to trust you on this endeavor. Anyhow, I just thought you'd like to accompany your old man this weekend to Atlantic City. I got a huge penthouse that is being paid for by Caesars and you're more than welcome to join me." Wow, was this a surprise. I'd actually love some quality time with my dad, and this emotion he was showing made me feel warm all over. To make things even better he said join "me," which meant that my step-mom was staying put in Vermont. Gambling with pops is too much fun to give up. I had to go. My pops often gambled in the seven figures, most often times in the negative side of the spectrum but nevertheless, all the perks that he got from being a high roller were too tempting to refuse. "Sure, I'll join ya dad," I told him. "Great. A limo will pick ya up 5 PM sharp this Friday. See ya in A.C, kiddo." Before I could go on my weekend rendezvous, I had to stop by the agency for a shoot with Dom. I was an elite model. I thought to myself that if the contract says be there at 2 PM, I could easily come in at three. I got to the shoot at 3:40 PM, an hour and forty minutes late. I had expected the glitterati to be nonchalant with my tardiness, but oh was I mistaken. "Well, who the fuck do you think you are? You spoiled little brat, I am officially through with this high and mighty persona you attempt to emit," one of the glitterati yelled. "Oh yeah, well who the fuck are you? Do you know who I am? I'm one of your biggest models ya old queen!" That was a mistake. The old dude I snapped at turned out to be the head of the agency that employed me. "Congratulations, young man. You are now officially blacklisted from ever working in the city ever again, I assure you. Good day!" I was fucked! This was bad. I tried to catch up to the dude as he walked away, but security had promptly escorted me off the premises. What the fuck am I going to tell the old man? I got back to my loft, took out a few hundred dollars and went on an epic cocaine and ketamine rage. I was satisfied with the fact that Vlad had left and my loft was still in one piece. Thank God for the little things in life.

# X S... , X T C , X ' D

The limo arrived exactly at 5 PM. I was in no shape to go to Atlantic City. My drug binge left me tired, cranky, and craving more, but nevertheless I had made pops a promise and I couldn't back out of it. The driver was a cool dude. We spoke about how much the Rolling Stones and Led Zeppelin were more influential then the Beatles. The driver sure knew a thing or two about rock music, which garnered my respect. I couldn't keep up the conversation for too long, though. I tried my best to perk up with a mixture of Vodka and one of those contemporary energy drinks but it didn't help out much. Half way to AC I heard something on the local radio station, and I begged the driver to blast it to full volume. It was Depeche Mode's "Personal Jesus". This song had pumped me up more than those bullshit energy drinks I had consumed. Just when I heard David Gahan's voice crescendo on the "reach out and touch faith" line, I became a new man. I had an emergency rail of cheech left over, so to celebrate I rolled up the divider between the driver and myself and snorted it. That's the problem with coke. It makes you feel like superman for a moment, and then makes ya feel as if superman shot up kryptonite. I felt like an annoying kid constantly asking the driver "Are we there yet?" Finally, we were minutes away from Excessville, or Atlantic City, whatever floats your boat. Caesars Palace felt like home to me. My father had been a gambler since I could remember. I checked my bag and went to the Casino to meet up with him. I knew exactly where I would find him: the V.I.P high roller baccarat tables. My dad always thought he was James Bond. He even drove a classic 1972 Aston Martin DBS just like Bond himself. The minimum bet at these tables was $1000. I glanced over and saw my pops, and looked like the old man was on a hot streak. "Hey Kiddo you're just in time to watch your dad bankrupt this sad sack of a casino." He was up around $800K at that point. "I'll stop as soon as I get to a cool Million, boyo." Sure enough, within minutes he had reached his goal. "C'mon. Daddy's gonna treat you to some prime aged fillet mignon." We went over to the local 5-star restaurant and ordered a pair of hundred dollar chops. I had absolutely no appetite whatsoever, but gave it my best to consume half of the steak. "You're getting too skinny son. Are you on something? I know you models have to watch your shapes, but this is getting ludicrous!" "No dad, I'm just super stressed with all this shit." "Language!" "Ah, sorry dad, but I am seriously stressed out with everything." "You think you're stressed out? I had to borrow a million smackeroos from the local mob just to pay our mortgage, your bills, and your step-mom's expensive tastes." "Wait what? Are we broke, pops? I mean gambling as much as ya usually do..." "You know what I always say kiddo, play checkers, concentrate on the now. I'm living for the moment, the here and now. I'm sure things will fall back into place for us. If they don't, well I'll keep up this stoic demeanor and no one will figure out we're fucked." "So what happens if ya lose the money pops? What are we going to do from now?" "Well, you have your job, so I'm going to stop supporting you. It's about time, if you ask me. All of my colleagues are flabbergasted by the fact that I pay for every little utility you have. I have a twenty-something year old bum, but a bum with a platinum spoon in his ass! Your mom has been begging me to stop supporting you for years, and now that you actually have some sort of a career I can finally cut you off in peace. I have my own troubles to deal with, boy." "Dad, that's the thing I was going to talk to you about." "I don't want to hear it! Do what you want with your life: fuck, snort, smoke, shoot up. Whatever. I don't know what they're teaching you in New York but just leave me out of it. Believe me son; I have more problems right now then a pregnant prostitute. Now excuse me, I'm going to hit the tables for a few more hours. I have to powwow with a few major players soon." After the conversation with pops, I had seriously contemplated jumping off the fucking roof and teaching the old man a thing or two. Luckily for me, the windows don't open up anywhere in Atlantic City, for obvious reasons. Fuck this shit! I'm in AC, I'm young, hot and I am going to enjoy myself before I have to go back to NYC penniless, blacklisted, and looking for an, ugh, NORMAL job. I had a hundred or so bucks in my wallet and hit the casino. A shady cat sitting by the bar offered me a cigarette and subtly implied that he was a proprietor of some very pure MDMA. I thought that the only logical thing to do was pick up some XTC that I could actually enjoy for hours instead of dropping a hundred on blackjack within minutes. He gave me an inside deal on the pills, six for a hundred. Luckily, it was Friday night and AC had some clubs that I could have fun in with my newly found supplies. I went back to the penthouse and changed. There would be no more flannel shirts, no more ray-bans and no more skinny jeans! Instead, I put on an overpriced Italian pink silk dress shirt, slacks and polished designer dress shoes. I pounded a shot of Vodka and popped all six pills with one swoop. I strolled to the nightclub getting looks from just about everybody who I came in contact with. The only thing missing was Puffy singing "Mo' money mo' problems" behind me. The clubs in New Jersey are similar to the ones in NYC. Overpriced drinks, girls who are not nearly as hot as they think they are, and douche bag guys in their late twenties and thirties trying to pick up a "10" but happily settling for a "-4". The pills hit me in one immense eruption. I think I might've seized for a moment, probably looking like an epileptic Japanese boy watching Pokémon for the first time. This shit was strong! I had begun to sweat profusely, and found myself losing my newly found stoic persona. I started to bump and grind with everyone on the dance floor. Some of the Jersey Guidos took offense to this and pushed me out of their radius while throwing a few fag bombs my way. I couldn't give a shit; I was on fucking cloud nine. The hours of utter bliss quickly made way to what I would predict to be at least two days of utter despair. The worst part of ecstasy isn't the actual crash, but rather the exact moment when you feel yourself very slowly coming down from the apex. The escalation to the pinnacle is surreal, but the moment when you realize that there is nowhere left for ya to go but down is traumatic. This is the story of my life, right? I reached the echelon and now am freefalling passed mediocrity and straight into rock bottom. It's 6 AM and I am barely able to keep myself from crying. The pain of the last couple of days is beginning to manifest itself within the fibers and sinews of my very being. My drug use, my fall from modeling grace, my family losing its money; this shit is seriously going to kill me. Top things off with the fact my serotonin has evaporated and I should stay away from anything sharp. For the ninth time in two weeks, I try to sleep, and for the ninth time in two weeks those plans fail. Just when I begin to dose off, a loud knock on my door makes me jolt up. "This is the police! Open up the door please." What the fuck is going on now? I don't think I did anything illegal last night, except for buying the MDMA. But if that dude was a narc, he would've simply arrested me on the spot. No, this can't be right. "Just a moment," I tell them and put on the complimentary robe as my shivering, dilapidated body inches towards the door. I crack the door open and see two leviathan cops. "May we come in, Sir? We have some bad news." "Sure," I say, and let them into the room. "Young man, there seems to have been an incident. "What happened?" "Sir, there is no easy way to tell you this, but your father was dealing with some bad people and..." "And what?" "He was found dead outside of the Borgata at around 5:45 this morning. We are sorry. Is there anybody you could call to pick you up?" "GET OUT, JUST GET THE FUCK OUT OF HERE!" This had to be a joke. I'm a good person. I fuck up and do bad shit, but only to myself. Why would God or Buddha or Moses or whoever is up there be doing this shit to me? I down the remaining half bottle of Vodka that's in my fridge and call Raya up. I tell her what had transpired. "Don't go anywhere Sniff. I'm getting Mikey, and we're heading up to AC to pick ya up." The hours I was left by myself in that God damn room waiting for Raya and Mikey were excruciating. I had become this misanthropic remnant of the person I thought I once was. I loathed everything and everyone, most noticeably myself. I hated Atlantic City, I hated the fucking Mob, I hated my dead father, and I hated this fucking cheesy, free cum stained bathrobe! How the fuck could shit go down like this? What the fuck was I supposed to do now? I couldn't help thinking about my step-mom and just how fucking elated she was when she'd hear that pops is dead, with all that insurance money going her way. She probably convinced dad to change his will and make sure she had received everything. "Oh honey, your son is a successful model, but what will happen to little ole me? I can't possibly work." I could hear her saying those words; I should fucking kill that cunt! A few hours passed by and Raya and Mikey finally picked me up. No one said anything, not even loud mouthed Mikey. The only positive thing of this experience was that now I could finally sleep.

" Home is where the heart is," they say. If that's the case, then I had an aortic aneurysm a decade ago!

I must've slept for a good three days before the phone had finally woke me up. "Hey kid, the funeral is tomorrow. Come if you want, if not then whatever." I can't believe that stupid cunt had the gall to call me! Not only was I going to make sure I was at that funeral, but I had a few things to tell Miss 1982 pageant queen. I offered Mikey three-hundred bucks to escort me to Vermont. He blatantly refused any money, and said that I could pay him in pot and munchies. The drive up to my old home was kind of nostalgic. Once we actually got up into Vermont, I recalled many of the drug hazed memories from the times I had once experienced in this quaint state. That's where I tripped on Acid for the first time, Mikey." "Oh yeah ma' dude? Let's trip again. Here, take this!" What better of a way to make an appearance at my dad's funeral then having a head full of acid? By the time we got to the cemetery I was tripping balls. A bunch of my old friends were present which meant a lot to me. I introduced Mikey to all of my old stomping ground buddies, and they automatically clicked. Now was the hard part: seeing my step-mom. "C'mon kiddo, I have to tell you something," she told me. "So here's the deal, kid. Your dad left just about everything to me, the estate and all of the assets. That being said, I'm pretty much not getting any of it because the old fuck has debts up to his ass, and I'm not going to go down like he did. Long story short little man, both of us are fucking broke!" This did not shock me; I was actually proud of my old man. I didn't get a dime of his estate, but at least this repulsive hag wasn't going to get anything herself. She could've run with the money, but the paranoia of her getting iced would keep her straight. I was peaking when they lowered my dad's coffin into the ground, ashes to ashes and all that jazz. Surprisingly, Mikey was having a worse trip then I was. I had been surprisingly serene during this whole experience. "How are ya doing through all of this, ma' dude?" he asked me. "Well, a numb soul can't be shocked." This brought a tear to his eye. "Don't say that, man. Just don't ever say that again, please." The funeral went by pretty quickly. A couple of my old buds invited Mikey and I back to their homes to partake in some illicit substances, but both of us refused simultaneously. There was nothing left for me in Vermont. My home was back in NYC, and I wanted to get back soon. "C'mon Mikey my man, let us head back towards civilization. I want to make it back for the Yankee game tonight. Andy Petite is pitching and I want to see him pick off a couple of noobs off first base." "Yeah, that sounds like a good idea dude." Pretty much the only thing I had left was my infatuation with the Yanks. That and of course, my two friends. "I'm taking ya clubbing tonight Sniff ma' man, ya deserve it." "Thanks Mikey, that sounds like a legit plan." We got back into Mikey's Nissan and blazed back to NYC. The LSD was gone and finally I shed a tear for my father. Maybe I wasn't completely numb after all. FUCK!

# C lubbing with D ouches/
# R ay of light.

The absolute last thing I should have been doing in my frame of mind was going clubbing, but I figured that it would've been better for me to be around friends right now then god forbid be by myself. Mikey dropped me off my loft and waited for me to shower and change. Raya met up with us a few minutes later. "Are ya Ok, Sniff? I know that's a retarded question, but ya know what I mean hun." "Yeah, I'll survive. I always do." Vlad couldn't come with; he had some soiree in Sheepshead Bay to go to, good riddance!" I changed into some dapper attire: a two-thousand dollar custom suit and Prada aviator shades. Raya was shocked to see that I was no longer a hipster. "Wow, ya clean up swimmingly there, stud." "What can I say? When life gives ya lemons, turn them into Gucci." Mikey went off to his car and brought back well over an 8-ball of cocaine. "Uncle Mikey has been saving this for a special occasion, kiddies. What better way is there for me to christen the white then with my two best buds and 80's night at Pacha?" Three heads to an 8-ball could be dangerous, I thought for a moment, but then realized I didn't give a shit. My dad's death had left me as a penniless orphan. I could find about ten things to justify me tailing out of control for a bit. We began to insufflate this fine Colombian product, and after only three or so lines Raya had begun to show some hesitation. "Nah girlie, youz finishing your share before the night is done, Uncle Mikey is gonna see to that!" By the looks of things, she really didn't look that into it, but whatever. I got my own problems to deal with. Cheeched out to the brink of seizing, we got into Mikey's whip and trekked our way to Pacha. I forgot who said it, but he was dead on: if you're over 25 and still clubbing, you're a complete douche bag! The line to get into the club was as long and winding as a Frost poem. Retarded coked out dildos were pushing each other to get in and groove to the eardrum-piercing beats of the dumbass DJ's. Both Raya and Mikey knew the main promoter, so we got in within a few minutes and got escorted straight into the VIP section. A bottle of Belvedere was waiting for us on our private table. "Let's get crunked, kiddies!" Mikey exclaimed and indeed crunked we got. We kept making impromptu trips to the bathroom to snort Mikey's cocaine. Raya skipped a few rounds but nevertheless got in quite a handful up her nose. The combination of Vodka and cocaine made me feel volatile. I was looking to fight somebody, anybody. Mikey was always feet from me just in case I snapped. The scene was truly pathetic. I hated everyone here. Every clubber was as fucking fake as silicone breast implants. I can't believe what I had turned into. A few weeks ago, I was a happy go lucky hipster, and now I was a douchey twenty-something club monkey. Fuck my life! I was so busy watching the dancing cocksuckers twirl and mack it to girls that I hadn't noticed that Raya was passed out cold in her seat. By the time both Mikey and myself went over to ask Raya if she was Ok, she was as cold as witch's tit. "Yo girl, stop playing around and come dance with Sniff and Uncle Mikey." Raya wasn't budging at all. I yelled into her ear that she was being a total killjoy but still she remained dormant. After a few more failed attempts at trying to resurrect Raya, Mikey and I glanced at one another. We didn't have to say anything; we knew what was transpiring here. The night on Pluto should've been a telltale sign that her body didn't cope with cocaine absorption too well. We had killed her! "Oh. My. Gawd. Sniff, what the fuck is going on right now, brother?" "Ya fucking killed her ya death mongering ass pirate! Ya killed Raya!" Don't you dare fucking pin all this on me! You're just as responsible man." "I'm responsible!?! What the fuck is wrong with you?" "Oh man dude, we're in some seriously deep shit right now." Mikey ran to the bathroom to flush down whatever cocaine he still had left, and I ran over to the bouncer screaming for help. The paramedics were always on call at a place like Pacha, but they were too late. She was pronounced dead on the spot from a Cocaine overdose. After the mandatory interrogation from the authorities I hailed the first cab and headed back to my loft. Mikey attempted to call me a plethora of times and sent a dozen or so texts but I quickly blocked his number out. This had to be it; this had to be that fucking rock bottom I had always heard about. There is no way I had anywhere left to go then up from here on now. I mean, c'mon, I was so low that I could scrape my fucking knuckles on the abysmal pavement. My dad was dead, my best friend was dead, my other best friend was figuratively dead to me, I had no other family, I had no fucking money and I had no bloody aspirations! But I still had some semblance of optimism, and I knew that I had to build myself up in order to save myself from caving in on myself. I had to grab what was left of my existence by the balls or just fucking end this whole charade once and for all.

Andre Zemnovitsch

MOLLY IS RAVING MAD.
SOMETIMES, SHE'S REALLY HARD
**TO SWALLOW...**

...AND SOMETIMES,
SHE WILL SWALLOW **YOU!**

# Everybody gets a 2nd chance/ U E s... ethics/ Fuck it, the spiral is more fun right now !

Raya's untimely demise had ripped a chasm in my being. The one thing that was keeping me lucid throughout this tumultuous ordeal was an essay that Raya wrote and had given me days before her overdose. It was titled The Convalescent Scenario, and the philosophy was pretty sound and applied itself flawlessly to what was going on around me. I had already established that I had hit rock bottom. With the untimely and brash deaths of my father and Raya, along with miscellaneous other detrimental peculiarities in my life that were plaguing me lately, her final words of wisdom were perfect. The Convalescent Scenario itself in a nutshell is a self-help manifesto for those who have plummeted to the brink of deterioration, like me. It tells the true story of one of Raya's close acquaintances, who had purposely had dwindled his physical, mental, and spiritual self to the brink of death. He was not masochistic or suicidal, just experimental. After starving himself for three or so days he had begun to hallucinate. He denounced all beliefs in terms of society, government and religion and according to him he was "now officially not a societal lemming." With the general appearance of an emaciated famine survivor and an inevitable onset of malaise, the grim reaper was even hesitant taking his soul. The gist of his neo-Gandhian experimentation was to focus and truly accentuate the positives of life while denouncing all negatives. In his warped perception, he believed that once one has hit rock bottom, but also simultaneously has cleared once soul and mind, then the convalescence and spiritual renaissance can finally begin, kind of like a modern phoenix. The last thing he wanted to do was perish but with his lack of nutrition and immunity, death was a very real possibility. He survived, and while building his being up to normality, all of the subtle tiers that he had climbed to reach mediocrity were unfathomably euphoric. When he had no more fear of death, when his hair had ceased to fall out, when his jaundice cleared, when his mind returned he experienced indescribable moments of jubilation that he would have never otherwise experienced if it hadn't been for the experiment. Eventually, he passed on from a drug overdose but as far as Raya knew it he had no regrets. "I go to bed with a smile on my face and wake up with a smile; I will not stop doing the things I love as long as I remain content. I would rather have thirty years of bliss then live a hundred of misanthropic malice." Makes you think a bit. Who is to say what's proper and what's not? I am sure a lot of us say that we don't care what anyone thinks as long as we think it's good, but yet people still sell their souls and discard their inherent beliefs. Bunch of bullshit con artists is who we are, and God knows I'm no different! I knew that there was no way I could go back to my old life nor could I go back to modeling, so pretty much I was screwed. Moments away from contemplating how I would off myself, I received an unexpected phone call from my father's old attorney. "Guess what kid? There was a glitch in the will, and you get $35,000. Put that money to good use, and once again my sincerest condolences for your loss." Holy shit dude! $35,000! I could do so much with that loot. I went over to the lawyer's office on Manhattan's Upper East Side to collect my cash and pondered what to do with it. Any rational person would invest most of it and use a small ration for food and shelter, but fuck it, I lost all rationality the moment I stepped foot in NYC. I was already on the prestigious Upper East Side of Manhattan when I had picked up my money so why not just get a hotel room there. I went over to the ritziest place I could find, and booked a month. The UES was packed to the teeth with pompous, arrogant old money ass clowns, but I couldn't give a flying fuck. I was a man on a mission. $18,000 down the drain, spent on the hotel. Oh well, I'm an optimist and that leaves me $17,000 to buy some well deserved necessities. My dealer asked me if I was kidding when I told him I wanted $15K of cocaine, speed and ketamine. I told him that I was dead serious and he met up with me. I could barely carry all of my new supplies back up to my hotel room. I had around $2000 left from my dad's will and around $450 I had stashed for a rainy day. That was it! I railed a good gram and a half of cheech and popped five Adderall to get a nice groove going. I decided to go to the last place I would ever go to with a clear head: Times Square!

# Times Square is Big Brother/ Central Park Ecosystem/ Fuck it all!

I really should've adhered to pops' advice and not play chess. I was merely a fucking pawn prostituting himself to suffice an addiction. All of the obscure rationale in the world couldn't convince me that things were not spinning out of control. I had a shit load of product at my UES hotel room but I knew that it would be gone soon enough. I had a little over two grand in cash left, but what the fuck was I to do once it had dissipated? I really am a fucking whore; spending the thousands my dad had left me to basically expedite my inevitable rendezvous with Beelzebub. I still had a few options left. I could sell the remaining drugs I had left and wisely invest the money into stocks and what not. Nah, that's just retarded. Why would I do something like that? I could get a normal job, maybe as a waiter. Nope, death seemed like a better alternative. I brought some cheech to Times Square with me. At this point, I probably had enough cocaine, speed, and ketamine to kill a bull elephant, but regardless I was a man on a mission! I hit a few bumps smack-dab in the middle of Times Square. I really couldn't give a flying fuck whether I would get incarcerated. Times Square is a fucking scary place by itself; add illicit substances to the equation and you're basically peering into hell itself. The first drug induced thought to scurry throughout my head was that if George Orwell was alive in today's day and age, his "Big Brother" archetype would be based on Times Square. Everywhere I turned I felt as if the buildings in the vicinity itself were eying me. All the billboards, monitors and bullshit overpriced tourist traps were following my every move. Even the Goddamn tourist scourges were after me. "Hey you take picture now!" some Japanese bloke had yelled at me. I promptly told him to go fuck himself and told him that I hoped Godzilla would sodomize his entire family. All of ya fucking tourists are a bunch of silly people, what with your morals and societal restraints. FUCK YOU! You're all a bunch of operatic clowns masquerading around in costumes made out of sinew and fiber, go back to decomposing like God had intended for you derelicts to do. My mind had begun to spin more and more out of normality. I had essentially turned into the Coney Island Ferris wheel; every rotation had become an epic struggle on my part. I truly began to detest the masses. I was built pretty solid but nevertheless coming to my end. The tourists masqueraded around Times Square like a gaggle of army ants on hallucinogens. I could not stand them any longer! I snorted the remnants of my cocaine and hailed the first cab back up to my pad on the UES. I knew this fuck would overcharge me, thinking I was a tourist. I couldn't blame him though; I was dumb enough to trek into this opalescent hellhole in the first place. I get back to my room and go on a binge of a lifetime. I nearly overdose at least a dozen times, and every time I fail to do so I get more and more aggravated. My stash is becoming non-existent. I have maybe half an 8-ball of cheech, a vial of ketamine, and three Addy's. I decide to go for broke and try this OD shtick one last time. It's all or nothing, motherfuckers! I rail the cocaine and ketamine simultaneously and every blood vessel in my already deviated nasal cavity bursts in one glorious hoorah. I pop the pills and hope to see the grim reaper. My surroundings begin to dissociate itself from the little reality I have a grasp on. As I get ready to see this proverbial light that everybody whispers about, I hallucinate that the grim reaper is standing by the threshold of my door. "Wow. You're too tweaked out for me to do anything with you, kid! I want no part of this shit!" That's all this hooded, bulimic fucktard has to say to me? What the Fuck?!? How pathetic am I? Not even death incarnate himself wants any part of dealing with me. I start coming back to life and decide to just shut my mind off completely. I'll give it 48 hours and if still feel like I have to leave this existence then that's what's going to be done! I finally get up around thirty hours later. Push is beginning to come to shove as I find myself in dire psychotherapeutic need. I'm out of drugs and pretty much the drugs I can purchase with the few schillings I have left will only be a tease. Maybe I should go out and find myself a nice corner in Chelsea, suck some cock and get some Meth. Fuck it, I'm not doing that. No, I'll die with dignity. Maybe I really should become a waiter? Nah I would rather suck cock, but think I'll do neither. I decide to give this squalor filled existence one final opportunity to try to convince me to stay in it a while longer. I build up the little remaining strength I have left and decide to take a stroll through Central Park. If this place can't convince me life is too beautiful to omit, then I am royally fucked. I walk down to the lobby and accidently catch my gaze in one of the mirrors. I look like a fucking zombie. My fault, I guess. All that shit I've been putting in my system will convert a beautiful guy into a walking cesspool. I walk over to the gates of Central park and take a deep elongated breath. Here I go; it's all or nothing time. At first I think I begin to feel some sort of reassuring feeling that maybe things will be alright. That all gets tossed aside when I gaze up into the sky and see the behemoth luxury skyscrapers looking down upon me. I feel as though I'm one of those microscopic organisms Dom had told me about and the skyscrapers are some sort of grandiose beings observing and mocking my every move. I begin to have a panic attack and run through the park. I bump into a few joggers and tourists and literally jump into the first opening I find. I'm fucked; I really can't handle this shit anymore! I can't be a bacterial presence in this existence but sadly that's what fucking fate had predetermined for me. I'm done; I'm going back to my sanctuary in the hotel and finishing it. Maybe fate will be kinder in resurrecting me into something more suitable in my next life, anything even an insect just not mere bacteria. I go back to my room and can't help but stare up into those horrendous monoliths overhead, judging me. Fucking vermin is what they are! I finally get back to the room, drenched in perspiration and dirty from jumping into the bushes. I get out the notepad in one of the desks and write something that will hopefully help explain my predicament to anybody that will take the time of day to actually read it. It's really happening; I seriously can't play this game any longer. I'm fucking done!

# May you all find solace

The moment that I understood my life was no longer linear was overwhelming. I woke up sweat stained and confused. Gasping for a breath that isn't there while the sun sears my retinas is hellish in every way. As I begin to convulse, I feel my limbs to prove to myself that all this is real. The hum of the alarm clock is relentless. Breakfast tastes awkward; its either 7 AM or 7PM, I don't fucking know! I cannot make sense of what is actually real and what I'm convincing myself is real. I crawl into the quintessential fetal position and rock myself back and forth trying to fathom what is going on. I grab a pen off of the floor and stab myself in my right middle knuckle. The pain hits me, and I smile because I still can sense. I am slightly amused that I instinctively use my left hand to pick up the pen, seeing as I am a righty. Everything in the room that consists of a darker hue is distorted. The ulcer-inducing hum in the background is ceaseless. My sense of smell and taste are completely gone, probably from the massive amounts of product that recently entered my body. I crawl onto my couch, feeling the leather and suede caress my skin. I imagine myself melding with it; I perceive myself as a tumor growing out of it. I cry myself back to sleep. I AM

NOTHING! Rats who feed off of decomposing carcasses are better and more beneficial to the world then me. At least they serve some purpose. I wish I was spring, sucking out winter's essence while converting the dismal blight into verdant splendor. But, alas, I am flawed and fated to fall. I have become what I feared most in this existence; a societal lemming! May you all find solace without me here.

-Sniff

# DUMBO

I felt their respect for me fall by the wayside as my bloodshot eyes sank into the meandering darkness. At one frail point of my life, reality was simply a preposterous entity. I serenaded perception the same way a playboy seduces a woman. I took to heart all the idiosyncratic nonsense that would identify me as a person, rather than just admit I'm a bacterial presence floating around in some deity's masterminded microcosm. I stepped gracefully to the edge of the warehouse roof in the DUMBO region of NYC. Ever since I first saw the view from the lower Manhattan skyline, I knew that this had to be the place I would end it. I was like a revered tightrope walker readying himself to take a bow before his adoring masses after accomplishing his daredevil's feat. Unfortunately, there was no one chanting my name or clapping, no one waiting for me down there. There was nothing but uncertainty. Never in my wildest dreams did I think it would ever come to this. I never grasped content to the point of actually commanding it consistently. As I do this blasphemous deed, I am reminded of the drug hazed tangent I had written on Raya's back. I close my eyes and see my best friend waiting for me in some undisclosed location. "Sorry things came to this Sniff, but Rayray will give ya a huge hug as soon as you cross." Tears begin to accumulate and I hear them bounce off of the far-off cement as delicately as a butterfly beats its wings. I spread my arms out, as if readying myself to fly. I look down onto the ground and see it morph into a dreadful darkness. I look straight onto the beautiful lower Manhattan panorama and begin to weep uncontrollably. There is so much beauty out there, all visible and heard, yet completely out of my grasp. The metropolitan skyline begins to turn into a chess board. At that instance I hear my father speak to me in the back of my psyche: "Fuck the chess players! Those who think more than one step ahead are merely a bunch of protozoan conmen who merely strive to fathom. Play checkers, son; concentrate on the now, not the 'what if.'" What do ya think I'm doing dad? The few words of advice he shared with me reverberate in my soul. As I hallucinate that the skyline is a chessboard, I ponder all the opportunities I wasted in my short life. I had it all and now I end up with a tear and a whimper. I hear Vlad and his goons cursing at me in Russian. I see Sveta shooting smack up, her arms organic topographic maps telling epic poems about her existence. I look at my arms and see nothing but bland simplicity. Should've done Heroin; it would've been cooler I think to myself, and smirk. I see Mikey spelling out words with Cocaine, and Dom shaking his head in disappointment. All the subway people are ridiculing me, everyone judging me, and rightfully so. I wait, and dare I say pray for God to tell me not to do this. Maybe give me a sign like in one of those inspirational Collective Soul videos. I wait for a white dove to land on my arm the moment before I plummet. Unfortunately the only thing that lands on me is some pigeon shit that scrapes my temple. You're one funny dude lord! I know this isn't a dream. I know I have to do this. Before I go off, I numb myself from everything. I stop crying, stop wondering, and stop trying to understand. I am stoic, finally! That's all you ever wanted Dad, for your good for nothing son to act like a stoic man. Well here it is,dammit! I don't know what's waiting for me on the other side. Maybe bliss, probably despair, but at this one moment in time, I couldn't care less. Enough! Let's do this, it's now or never! I jump off, and feel the gentle wind kiss my falling flesh. All is right for that moment, all is good. I am content, before the pavement reminds me once more that like a good ecstasy experience, what goes up, must inevitably crash down!

Andre Zemnovitsch